SAVING MEADOW

THE NEXT GENERATION
BOOK 1

RILEY EDWARDS

Saving Meadow
The Next Generation

This is a work of fiction. Names, characters, businesses, places, events, and incidents are either the products of the author's imagination or used in a fictitious manner. Any resemblance to actual persons, living or dead, or actual events is purely coincidental.

Copyright © 2022 by Riley Edwards

Cover design: Jena Brignola

Written by: Riley Edwards

Published by: Riley Edwards/Rebels Romance

Edited by: Cindy Wolken

Proofreader: Kendall Barnett

Book Name: Saving Meadow

SPECIAL EDITION

Paperback ISBN: 978-1-951567-33-0

First edition: December 26, 2022

Copyright © 2022 Riley Edwards

CONTENTS

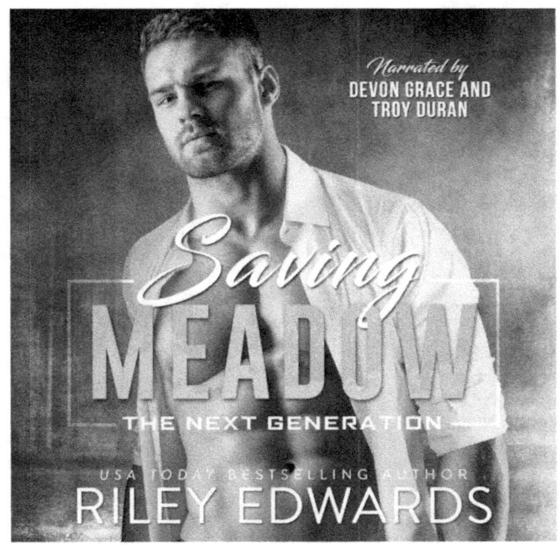

Performed By: Troy Duran & Devon Grace

PROLOGUE

"NICHOLAS, JUST IN TIME." Nick Clark turned, finding himself face-to-face with the man he'd come to see.

"Director," Nick greeted.

"How does it feel walking back in here with a shield and creds?" the director asked, offering Nick his hand.

"Different." Nick took his hand in a firm shake and contemplated his answer.

He did feel different. Not even two days ago he'd walked through these very doors with his family. That had felt different as well, sitting in the front of the graduation hall taking his final oath, alongside the men and women who'd become his comrades. They'd spent the last six months together, training both physically and mentally toward a common goal – the honor to call themselves *Special Agents.*

He'd vowed his service and allegiance, to protect and serve, to honor the office of the FBI. Nick had sworn fidelity, bravery, and integrity. Words he would never forget, the very words that were proudly carved above the entrance to FBI headquarters and every field office across the U.S.

Now, as he stood in front of the building shaking the director's hand, Nick felt the heaviness of his position weighing on him. All his life, Nick knew he wanted to serve, like his uncles. Only the military hadn't appealed to him. He'd watched the toll it took on his uncles: Clark, Lenox, Levi, and Jasper. Every mission they'd completed seemed to take another bite out of their souls. While the men that had raised him and been his mentors were strong enough for that type of service, Nick knew he wasn't. He wanted to help catch the bad guys, lock them up and keep the public safe on the homefront, not fight a war that was unwinnable – not in the immediate. Nick was far too impatient; he liked closure and control. He admired his uncles and knew their service was necessary and selfless, but he'd chosen a different path.

The FBI had been Nick's dream. He found every part of the criminal mind fascinating, and the process in which the offender was apprehended even more so. The investigation and progression of a case had sparked something deep in Nick at a very young age. He'd been lucky growing up with four men who had taught him to hone his instincts. They'd schooled him on battlefield tactics and weapons safety the moment he'd expressed an interest in law enforcement. His uncles had also walked him through the process of critical thinking and crime scene investigation. While his uncles may have been gathering intel on terrorists in a foreign country, the process was the same.

"Come on. We're meeting with Unit Chief Kilby. He should already be inside."

The director held open the door for Nick to precede him. Once both men were in the building, Nick fell in step beside the director. Instead of going to the second floor where Nick knew the other man's office was located, they continued further into the lobby before turning right and stopping in front of a set of double doors, frosted for privacy and *Behavioral Analysist Unit* etched in the glass.

Nick's brow knitted, and he wondered why the director was taking him to the BAU. Not that he would question the man; Nick wasn't dumb. The director scanned his badge and the lock clicked, allowing the men entrance into what he'd considered the Holy

Grail of the FBI, a place that he'd fantasized about being a part of, but knew it would take a master's degree and a decade of hard work to prove his worth before he'd even be considered. The badge clipped to his belt was still shiny and brand new. He couldn't even call it a shield yet, he'd only earned it two days ago. It was silly, but to Nick, it would be a badge until it had some scratches on it, until he could prove himself as a SA.

The room was exactly as he'd known it would be. Not the desks, or office furniture, or the file cabinets that lined the wall, or even the conference room he could see off to the side. It was the energy of the room; it was electric and alive. These men and women dug into the psyche and picked it apart, analyzing a criminal's behavior to reconstruct the unsub's motives, method, and the rationale behind the crime. In other words, Nick thought the profilers with the BAU were brilliant and maybe a little twisted themselves. After all, there had to be a price to pay climbing into the mind of a killer.

"SSA Kilby." the director greeted when they'd approached a tall man in his late forties. "This is SA Clark."

"Yes. Nice to meet you. Let's go into the conference room and talk."

"A pleasure." With a nod, Nick silently followed both men, scanning the office as he went.

When the men were seated around the table, SSA Kilby started. "The director tells me you were the top of your graduating class."

"That is correct, sir."

"Please call me Kilby, everyone else does. We're not big on formalities around here. The director gave me your file. I'm impressed."

"Thank you."

"You scored exceptionally well all around; however, it is the way you processed the mock crime scenes that truly interests me. In all the scenarios you found things your peers had missed. And you analyzed the evidence presented differently as well."

Kilby's praise struck Nick straight in the gut. He didn't often need validation from others but coming from SSA Kilby it meant something to him. However, Nick was mildly uncomfortable, and not knowing what to say, he remained quiet.

Kilby slid an image across the table to Nick. "What is the first thing that comes to mind when you look at that image?"

Nick looked down at the photograph of a grizzly crime scene; a male and female lying on the floor of a living room, blood pooling around their bodies, staining the carpet. Each had multiple stab wounds. At first glance, he'd say each had to have at least a dozen or more. He continued to scrutinize the image, looking for anything that stood out, nothing did. A family home, modest in the furnishings he could see. Nothing ransacked or displaced, both bodies still clothed, not posed.

"Why?" Nick asked.

"Why?" Kilby's brow pulled up, and he studied Nick from across the table. "Interesting. Explain your question."

"When I look at the crime scene the first thing I want to know is why. Why them? Why that house? Why did the offender use a knife? Why the overkill? What drove the unsub? Once I start there, I can work backwards through the solution matrix. It is easier to build on what I don't know then find the who, what, where, and when. The *why* is what tells the real story."

Kilby and the director exchanged a look before Kilby retrieved a file from the storage credenza behind him. For the first time since Nick entered the room, he took the time to take in his surroundings. A modern black laminate table with brushed aluminum sides, eight high-back leather executive chairs, a matching black storage cabinet, a bank of monitors hung on one wall, a large gold FBI - BAU crest embellished the adjoining wall. Classy, clean, and efficient. Nick sat back in his chair willing himself still, uncertain of what was happening. Oddly he felt like he was in a job interview. Not knowing if he'd passed the impromptu exam or got the job – not that he understood what the job was - was driving him crazy, but he refused to fidget in front of the men.

"Do you know why you're here?" Kilby asked.

"No."

"There is an opening on my team, SA Winters is leaving. He's been asked to teach a class on the taxonomy of human behavior. The director and I have spoken at length about bringing you on the team as his replacement. A fresh set of eyes, no bad law enforcement habits to break, no preconceived bias. We can mold you into what we need. I still have my reservations. However, there is no denying you have a natural instinct that cannot be ignored. I'd like you to look at an ongoing investigation and present a profile and full report."

Before Nick could answer, a manila folder was slid across the table. Nick stopped the dossier with his hand, looking down at it. Once again, his chest filled with pride - Federal Bureau of Investigations: Case File 033077RE neatly stamped on the front. He opened the folder, and his heart rate spiked, and not from the excitement of perusing his first official case. He thought about closing the file and taking a minute to mentally prepare for the image that had assaulted him. He stared at the crime scene photo - a woman lay dead in an alley. Dark hair, age unknown due to multiple stab wounds to her face, height, and weight indeterminable. Nick flipped the image, and the next photograph was worse. A blonde woman, again in an alley; this woman's face was peeling and blistered, her features and age uncertain. Nick flipped through more pages, all women, all with facial disfiguration; blondes, brunettes, red heads, and black hair. All white, all dumped in the open.

When he got to the last image, he turned it over and looked at the men, carefully studying him.

"Eleven women over twelve months," Kilby started. "You'll find the rest of the information at the desk I had cleared for you. I'll introduce you to the team and let you get to work."

What the fuck had just happened? Nick gawked at the unit chief and hoped his mouth wasn't actually hanging open in his stupor.

"Thank you for the opportunity," Nick stammered. "When would you like the profile?"

"Tomorrow. You'll present it to the team at 9 a.m."

Tomorrow? Was Kilby insane? He'd need more

than twenty-four hours to properly comb the case and research the terminology and theories he still didn't grasp. He still had so much to learn, ten years' worth of knowledge to be exact, that was the average time it took before an agent was considered.

"Don't over think this. I don't want a textbook profile. I have four highly qualified profilers that have already worked up a report. I want your gut feeling. Tell me the why. Think outside the box."

"I don't know what the box is in this case."

"The box is the textbook profile, look past it. Tell me what we don't know. That's how we'll find this son of a bitch. Stop thinking like Special Agent Nick Clark and get in the killer's head; feel it, experience it, what's the fantasy. Then you'll have your composite of the offender."

Wordlessly, Nick stood when the other two men did and followed them back into the central office. Three men and a woman were standing near an empty desk, their conversation coming to a halt as the three men approached.

"Nick Clark this is, Mike Gonzales, Joel Brinkley, Ben Dailey, and Mandy Brown. Your new team."

And that was the beginning of Nick's trial by fire and unconventional introduction to the BAU.

1

Deface

FOUR YEARS LATER.

"Hey, Nick. Conference room," Mike told me as he passed by my desk.

"What's going on?" I asked as I fell into step.

"No idea. Hope you're not too hungover from last night," Mike chuckled. "We have a new case."

I barely resisted the urge to rub my temples now that Mike had me remembering how much I drank last night. Four years ago, when I'd joined the BAU, Mike had been my harshest critic. He also took the longest to accept me as part of the team. While I understood his apprehension, it still had pissed me off, and we'd bumped heads — and that was putting it mildly. I can credit most of my improvement over the years to his careful examination and assessment of my work. Once I'd proved to have potential, Mike took me under his wing and mentored me. He was also my closest friend at the Bureau.

Mandy, Joel, and Ben were already sitting around the conference table when Mike and I walked in.

"Surprised to see you this morning after all the shots you did," Mandy jabbed.

"Shit, you outdrank Ben last night, and that's unheard of," Joel added.

Ben was known to hold his liquor. He also had expensive taste, meaning I'd spent a small fortune last night buying rounds.

"The Boy Wonder has finally grown a pair of balls," Ben added his two-cents.

Mike clipped me on the shoulder as he took his seat. "Boy Wonder. Haven't heard that in a while. And to think when we got you, you were barely old enough to drink."

Over the years, I'd heard it all, but Boy Wonder was their favorite nickname. Mike wasn't wrong. When I'd joined the team I was twenty-two, the youngest by nearly twenty years.

SSA Kilby entered the room with Kristy, our technical analyst, and the joking came to a stop.

"We have a new case. Local law enforcement has requested our help due to the brutality of the kill - I've agreed," Kilby said and took his seat at the head of the table while Kristy turned on the wall monitor.

When the screen came to life, a crime scene photo appeared. Brutal didn't quite describe the image. The woman was a mangled mess. The level of violence screamed extreme rage.

"Lauren Marshall, twenty-four, single, worked as a book publicist," Kristy started and switched the image on the screen to her driver's license photo. "She was last seen at Cheers, an upscale wine bar in Woodbridge. Her friends told police they'd met there after work for a drink. Lauren stayed to listen to the Jazz band, which wasn't unusual for her to do. Her body was found in a parking lot less than a block away."

Shit, Woodbridge was less than twenty minutes from Quantico. Despite what TV dramas about the FBI portrayed, it was rare we went to the crime scene. It's not possible for local police to keep a body at a crime scene for the length of time it would take us to get there. We relied on law enforcement to collect evidence and present it to the team. But, with this kill being so close, there was a likelihood Kilby would want to go to the site.

"Toxicology?" Mike asked.

Kristy looked up from her tablet to answer, "Ketamine."

"Offical cause of death?" I asked.

"Exsanguination. I've emailed you all the report," Kristy said.

"No sexual assault," Ben noted as he scanned the information on his tablet.

"Stab wounds to the abdomen and face," Mandy added.

Stab wounds was barely scratching the surface; Lauren's face was demolished. She was unrecognizable.

"Only one stab wound to the lower abdomen. No sexual assault. Face annihilated. Ketamine. Exsanguination." I listed some of the facts of the case.

"I know where you're going with that. You think he's back," Mike said.

"Copycat?" Ben asked.

"The ketamine was never released to the public," Mandy piped up.

"Four years between kills," Kilby added.

"After body eleven and the seventh of the following month passed we'd assumed he'd been locked up on other charges," I reminded him of our initial profile. "The Butcher is back."

The Butcher was my first case with the BAU, and

four years later it was unsolved. The offender had up and vanished. Eleven kills, all on the seventh day of the month, all dumped in a public location, all had ketamine in their system; all had a single stab wound in their lower abdomens, their faces disfigured, nothing taken, nothing left. The new homicide fit the victimology. Pretty woman mid-twenties, low-risk lifestyle. The common factor was they were all what society would consider beautiful.

Today was the twentieth of the month.

The wait had begun.

2

Pretty Face

"GOOD MORNING, MEADOW." Beth stopped at my desk, her eyes went wide, and I braced for what would come next. "Oh, I'm happy you finally decided to stop trying to cover up the awful scar. By the end of the day, your make-up just wears off and you can see it anyway. It's such a shame; you were such a beautiful girl. I mean you still are, even with the scar on your face." Beth smiled a bright smile as she continued by my desk as if she wasn't just a royal bitch.

Who says that?

Beth does, that's who. And most everyone else. At least she makes comments to my face instead of whispering them behind my back. I should've been used to it by now. From the moment I'd woken up in the hospital with this hideous scar marring my face, people have been making comments.

Oh, you poor thing.

Does it hurt?

So sad to mark such a pretty face.

I've heard it all, and mostly I ignored the stares and running commentary about how my scar came to be. People comment as if I don't know I have a six-inch scar running from my ear to my chin. I knew it was there; I saw it every day. A stark reminder that I was lucky to be alive. My flesh had been flayed open with such force two of my teeth were dislodged, and I have dental implants. Unfortunately, even after plastic surgery, the scar was still prevalent.

These days I chose to view the mark as a symbol of what I lived through. I've not always felt that way. There were many dark days after the attack happened. I was too afraid to leave my house, horrified I looked like a monster, and there was a time I'd contemplated ending it all. I might've if it wasn't for a very special woman, who'd I clung to like a lifeline. Veronica-Venus21 was my savior even though I'd never met her in real life. She was a member of a message board I joined after I was released from the hospital. The group was for victims of violent crimes. We'd spent hours in the online chatroom. She'd survived a horrific ordeal, much worse than mine, and she'd made it through. She gave me hope.

"Good morning to you, too, Beth. I put your new sales reports on your desk." I flashed what I hoped was a normal-looking smile. Because in my mind I had jumped on her back like a spider monkey and knocked her to the ground, banging her pinchy face into the cheap Berber office carpet.

Bitch.

By the time lunch rolled around, I was ready to go home. Monday mornings always sucked, but this one was especially craptastic. My normally mild-mannered, sweetheart of a boss, was tired and crabby. She had only been back from maternity leave for a month, and her new baby had colic, which in non-parent layman's terms meant *I am miserable, so you will be too.*

I'd normally work through lunch, snacking at my desk, but today I had to get some fresh air. The entire office seemed to be off. I grabbed a turkey sandwich from the sub shop next door and sat on one of the benches out front and just as the deliciousness that was a turkey on rye with extra swiss and extra mustard was at my lips, Rory plopped down beside me.

I jumped, squeezed, and mustard shot out of the

bottom of my yummy sandwich at the speed of light, and now I was wearing it, a huge yellow spot on the front of my teal blouse.

"Shit. Sorry, Meadow," she stammered and proceeded to molest my breasts with a napkin, further smearing the offending condiment into the material.

I will admit for a moment I did contemplate the fact that in the past five years, my co-worker had been the only person to touch my breasts; and how sad that detail was. I was twenty-six years old and hadn't had a single sexual experience with anyone in years – until Rory and her exploring hands.

"It's fine." I stilled her hands and took over, but it was too late. The stain was huge now, spreading nipple to nipple instead of smack dab in the middle of my chest.

"Today sucks," Rory huffed.

"You're telling me."

I was going to smell like a hoagie all day.

"It's like a case of the body snatchers on my floor today. Everyone is acting like assholes," she complained.

Rory worked on the floor above mine in the accounting department. She was nice enough, but our paths rarely crossed.

"Oh good, it's not just the sales team then. I

thought they'd all been infected with douche canoe virus."

"You know, me and some of the girls from HR are going to happy hour tonight. You should join us."

Memories of the last time I went to happy hour flooded and the panic that accompanies those thoughts rose to the surface with such force I physically jerked, dropping my sandwich on the ground.

"Fudgesicle."

"Shit girl, are you okay?" Rory asked.

"Yeah. I just remembered I didn't finish Beth's weekly sales forecast. She'll be pissed. I gotta get back to the office." I tried to cover up my freakish reaction to her mentioning getting drinks.

Then I did what I always did when the memories of that night became too much. I sent a message to Veronica Venus.

3

The 20th

"KYLIE PETERS, twenty-two, five feet one, one hundred ten pounds." Mike looked up from the girl's license and shook his head. "Poor thing didn't have a chance."

The young woman looked smaller than her five-feet-one lying crumpled on the cement behind Lucky's Bar. It was the twentieth, and the local PD had called the team to the scene before they'd moved the body. Rot and decay from the nearby dumpster masked the coppery smell of the pool of blood around the victim's head. Thirty puncture wounds in the face and one knife wound to the lower abdomen.

The area was a mess. Bystanders looked on; some

tried to take cell phone pictures and video. What the fuck was wrong with people? A woman was dead, and all some people could think about was posting the images on their twitter feed. The alley was too small to pull the ambulance in, not that it was needed, but protocol dictated EMS still answer the call. It sat at the curb next to the medical examiner's van. Blue and red lit up the area like a beacon for all to see. So much for keeping these latest murders from the media. They'd be here next, no doubt.

"Christ," I muttered. "Looks like she took an ice pick to the face." Not having the stomach to look at what was left of her face, I moved to look around the area that had been marked off with yellow crime scene tape. No murder weapon, no trace blood leading away from the body, nothing. Two new bodies and we were no closer to catching the offender.

"You ready to head back?" Mike asked. "The rest of the team is loading up."

"More than."

The drive back to the office was filled with Mike lamenting how his ex-wife was now dating. Their divorce had only been finalized recently, and he'd been holding out hope for reconciliation, even after the judge stamped the final decree. They'd been married eighteen years and had three girls, and now Mike found himself alone in an apartment he hated while his ex and the kids remained in the family home.

Mike parked the SUV and turned to me. "I never thought I'd be forty-two years old and starting over. I haven't been on a date in twenty years. You know what she said when she left? She needed a fresh start. I've been with the BAU for almost ten years. I have a master's in psychology. Years' worth of training in behavioral science and I still don't know what the fuck that means. What signs did I miss?"

"I don't know. Are you sure you missed the signs?" I asked.

"What the hell does that mean?"

"It means you don't miss much. You've seen more than the rest of us. Ask yourself, did you miss it, or did you ignore it? I've never been married; I'm not the right person to talk to about this. But I do have four aunts, and when they were upset, there was no missing it. So, either your ex was a master of deception, or you didn't want to believe the woman you've spent half your life loving was capable of stepping out on you."

"You're an asshole."

"That may be true. I've been called that a time or two. But, it doesn't mean I'm wrong. What Donna did was completely fucked. What she's doing now is wrong." I didn't want to hurt Mike, but he had to pull his head out of his ass about his ex. "She's not your concern, Mike. You have three beautiful girls. They're what is important now. Show them how much you love them. Focus all of your energy on them, and you'll be golden."

"How did you know Donna had an affair? I never told you that."

"Seriously? She's textbook. Statistics show that the likelihood a woman will divorce, especially women in long-term marriages, strongly correlates with her preconceived ability to remarry. Women initiating divorce after the age of forty with children is low unless there is abuse or some other stressor. I know there's not abuse in your home. No job loss, no death of a close relative, no sick child. That leaves another man - her fresh start. You may have wanted to keep your head in the sand, but the signs were there. The new hairstyle, the new clothes. You bitched about her running the cards up to get those things. The gym. Really, you missed all that?"

"I'm afraid to ask why you know divorce rates," Mike said.

"Women fascinate me. You grow up hearing sayings like happy wife, happy life. There are poems written about women scorned, songs about women burning an ex's house down. What makes a woman both the loving nurturer and so emotionally unbalanced she can key your car and toss your shit on the front lawn all in one afternoon. Women provide care, feed their young, cuddle and love. But there is nothing fiercer than a mama bear when her young are threatened. They are ruthless and merciless. Kipling wrote, '*Her contentions are her children, Heaven help him who denies. He will meet no suave discussion, but the instant, white-hot, wild, wakened female of the species warring as for spouse and child.*'."

"Son, don't ever call a woman emotionally unbalanced to her face or you'll find more than your shit on her front lawn. You can take that advice to the bank." He chuckled, and in true Mike fashion, when he's done with a conversation, he ended it, without preamble. He was out of the SUV, already walking toward the office before I caught up with him.

He beeped the locks and mumbled his thanks.

———

WE WERE MISSING SOMETHING. Thirteen bodies and still no trace evidence had been left behind. The profile needed to be reworked.

One white board had crime scene photos too gruesome to look at; the other had the timeline and photographs obtained from DMV records. There was a connection; we were overlooking it.

"Why?" I asked the room. "Why these women?"

"They were convenient, easy targets. All had alcohol in their system at the time of death," Ben answered.

"None over the legal limit," Mandy clarified.

"We've established the offender is sexually incompetent. Small in stature, the unsub needs the ketamine to incapacitate the victims; he can't otherwise overpower them on his own. Unassuming, non-threatening, and even friendly. The women all left willingly. Even with the overkill and rage, suggesting revenge or jealousy, the kill is still controlled. He only mutilates the face and a single stab wound to the abdomen. Organized, mid to late twenties," Joel read the profile.

"The first eleven were killed on the seventh. The last two on the twentieth. Why the change in the day of the month?" I mused.

"The stressor changed. We thought there was a childhood trauma that had occurred on the seventh day of a month. The change in the day now suggests the trauma occurred in adulthood. Something recent," Mike surmised and thumbed through the file in front of him.

"The ketamine? Mandy, was there a change in the toxicology report?" I asked.

"No change. Administered orally, the high dose would take effect approximately ten minutes after it was ingested," she answered.

"The only change is the stressor." I stopped and checked my watch; 4 a.m., too early to call in our tech Kristy. "When Kristy comes in, we'll have her run the seventh of the month going back a year from the first batch of murders. Anything newsworthy. And for the twentieth going back four years. We need to find what is so important on those days."

"I'll run doctors prescribing ketamine again." Joel stood and added. "Ben, where are we on the security camera in the bar?"

"Same as the others. The day of the murder has been wiped clean," he answered.

"I'm going home to get a few more hours sleep." Mandy tried to stifle her yawn and rubbed her eyes. "I'm too old for this."

"Me too." I gathered my files and picked up my cell and tablet before heading for the door. "I'll see you all in a few hours."

I didn't bother stopping by my desk to secure my files. I knew I wouldn't be able to sleep; I might as well use the quiet early morning hours to sift through them.

We were missing something big. The clock was ticking until we found another mangled body in the alley. The BAU didn't catch killers, the local police officers did. The profile was an investigative tool, one that helped the police narrow their suspect list and save man-hours, and hopefully lives. The problem with this case was the police didn't have any suspects. The team was putting in extra hours trying to nail this guy. The more information we could provide the PD, the faster this animal could be locked away.

I was dog-ass tired by the time I pulled into my driveway. The early morning coffee and adrenaline had worn off. I needed a nap; then I'd look through my notes again. I opened my door and went in search of my girl, Sally, and my bed.

4

Nightmares and java

"PLEASE DON'T DO THIS," *Meadow begged.*

"You think because you're so pretty you can have whatever you want. Take and take. Steal what doesn't belong to you."

"I don't. I promise. I didn't steal anything. Please don't," Meadow cried out in agony as her flesh was pierced. A rush of searing heat bloomed in her stomach and radiated outward until it engulfed her entire body. The rough cement scraped the skin on her back as she tried to escape the anguish that threatened to pull her under.

"You shouldn't take what isn't yours, you dirty bitch."

"Please," Meadow begged and tried to blink to clear the haziness.

The flash of a knife blade reflected the light from overhead and Meadow gave in to the pain; everything went dark.

The scream that filled the room was involuntary as I scrambled out of bed, landing on the floor with a thud. My legs were twisted in my sheet, which now was pulled clean off my bed, wrapping me in a sweaty cocoon.

Why was this happening again?

I'd gone almost a year without a nightmare. No, not a nightmare. Nightmares are scary dreams invented by your imagination. These were memories, my reality. My living hell.

A shower did nothing to wash away the lingering effects of my nocturnal torture. I hated I still couldn't stop myself from remembering what happened. Well, that wasn't true. I couldn't remember, not the most important part anyway. The police had interviewed me dozens of times, both in the hospital and the weeks after I'd been released. They couldn't understand how I couldn't remember my attacker's face. I couldn't even remember his voice. Nothing. Just the pain. I couldn't forget any of the pain. Not the stab to my stomach, not the weeks of fever and infection, and not the ache I'd felt when the doctor told me infection had severely damaged my reproductive system and I'd never have children.

I fucking hated remembering.

I yanked the rest of the bedding off the mattress, dragging the bundle to the tiny laundry area, and tossed it in front of the stackable washer and dryer. I'd deal with it later. The lingering smell of fear filled my small apartment and threatened to choke me.

I had to leave.

The trendy coffee house on the corner of my street gave me a measure of comfort. I've been coming here for years, ever since I'd moved to Virginia right before my attack. Strangely this shop was the one constant in my life. I waited in line, ordered, and took my creamy, vanilla-flavored yumminess from Becky, the purple-haired barista. Coffee in hand, I moved to the back of the small space to the table in the corner, all the while thinking how sad my life had turned out to be. I thought I'd be married by now, maybe have a baby on the way. I would've finished my degree and the only worry I'd have was whether I'd give up my career to be a stay-at-home mom. I totally would've. I had wanted kids, wanted to be a mother. Now that was gone, and what was left was nothing short of a tragedy. Instead of a man and a family, I had a coffee house and Becky. The girl had been working here since the first time I'd come in. The only thing about her that'd changed over the years was her hair color. She'd never treated me differently, even when I'd come in with the bandage on my face. The only comment she'd made was, *I hope they fry the bastard that hurt you.* Then she took my order and smiled.

The bastard that did this to me would never fry. He was never caught. He was free to walk around while I lived with the reminder of his brutality. I didn't need to look in the mirror to recall what my face looked like; I had the ugly scar committed to memory, every depression of my skin, the zig-zag where my flesh was sewn back together, the puckered edge near my ear. Worse than my face was the three-inch souvenir my attacker left on my belly. He'd left me barren, stolen my dreams, and made me half a woman.

A laugh from the table next to me pulled me from my miserable thoughts. Two men sat facing opposite each other. Both looked to have just finished a workout. The man laughing was the epitome of a Hollywood movie star. I'd seen him plenty. Sometimes he was in a suit, others in jeans and tee, I'd even seen him in his work-out clothes before. It didn't matter what Nick wore; he was absurdly good looking. I felt like a creeper sitting in my corner studying the man, but he was that hot. I couldn't look away; I never could. I even felt a little weird that I knew his name. But come on, it's a coffee house, when your order was up the barista called your name, and you picked up your order at the counter. I even knew he favored a Macchiato but sometimes ordered a frozen Vanilla Chai if it was warm out.

Five years ago, I'd almost talked to him. He was standing next to me waiting for his coffee and right when I had the nerve to say something his phone rang, and he answered it with a "hi sweetie." Of course, a man as sexy as Nick would have a wife or girlfriend. His voice had softened when he spoke, and I wished I had a man that would talk to me that way. Even before my attack, I'd been shy around men. Now? I avoid them like the plague. But that didn't mean I still hadn't studied Nick over the years. Each time I saw him I ached for a man like him - strong, handsome, and sweet. But I'd never have that. Who'd want a woman like me?

My phone chimed, and I looked at the screen. Smiling, I swiped it to display a message from Veronica Venus.

VV21: Happy Sunday.

The meme attached had me giggling. The picture

was of an angry cat and the caption read: When the coffee house changes staff, and they don't know your order.

Me: LOL. How'd you know I was at a coffee house? Creeper. hehe

VV21: It's Sunday, and you're predictable. You always visit the famous Sam's on the weekend.

Me: No, I don't. I visit the famous Sam's EVERY chance I get. The vanilla flavored goodness is the only happiness I have in my life.

I'd meant that as a joke, kinda. But Veronica Venus was too perceptive.

VV21: What's wrong?

Me: Nothing. Same ol' same ol'. Work was insane this week. Sorry I've been MIA.

VV21: Bullshit. Are you dreaming again? Dammit Meadow, why didn't you message me?

Sigh.

I didn't know Veronica Venus's real name. She knew mine but didn't know "Meadow" wasn't a made-up screen name. My name was unusual enough when I'd signed up for the survivor's message board I hadn't used a made-up moniker.

I knew she wouldn't give up until I spilled my guts, so I commenced telling her about my hellacious week.

I looked up from my phone in time to watch Nick

and his friend leave the coffee shop. Why did the back side of him have to look just as good as the front?

Hell hath no fury

IT WAS ALMOST THE TWENTIETH.

We were no closer to being able to provide the police with any new information. The thought of another woman facing a gruesome death at the hands of a sick and twisted killer had my gut in knots.

Joel had been able to track down twenty doctors in the tri-state area that had prescribed ketamine to treat patients with mental illness. Only five of them had been prescribing the drug for over five years. Ketamine was used to treat depression and bipolar disorder, but it was not a drug widely used. The side effects were horrible. Joel and Mandy had gone to interview the doctors and see if the doctors had any insight or useful information.

Kristy's search of the seventh and twentieth of the month had turned up nothing by way of news, which was helpful and told us that whatever had happened on those dates was personal to the offender.

Mike was at his desk angrily pounding on his laptop. The man was getting ready to snap. His ex had introduced the new boyfriend to his kids last night. The worst of it was she'd called Mike beforehand and told him that the deterioration of the marriage had been his fault. If he'd paid more attention to her, she wouldn't have had to look for it elsewhere. To add insult to injury, she admitted that she was rubbing Mike's face in her new relationship to show Mike what he'd thrown away.

Christ. The man looked devastated. I thought back to the conversation we'd had in the car. Women truly were fascinating. Soft, sexy, intelligent beings that could turn into vengeful blood-thirsty beasts at the drop of a dime.

My attention was drawn back to the images in front of me, the last two victims from the twentieth.

Vic one – single stab wound to the lower stomach. Stabbed in the face multiple times with the same weapon used on the abdomen.

Vic two – same stab to the stomach, only a secondary weapon had been used – an ice pick.

I looked back to the very first victim from nearly five years ago. She'd been killed the same way as vic one of the twentieth kills. Same weapon – knife to the gut and the face. Vic two and the second vic from the killings on the seventh didn't match. The second vic had a single stab, but her face had been burned with acid.

"Hey, Mike?" I called to get Mike's attention.

"What?" he barked.

Goddamn, the man was in a bad mood. Not that I blamed him, but we had five days until we'd find a new body. I needed his head in the case, not on the woman who was hell-bent on sticking it to his friend. Donna was taking her revenge for lack of attention to a whole new level. It was a tad bit overkill.

Revenge.

Overkill.

"We profiled that the offender was unassuming, non-threatening, and friendly enough that the women would leave the bar with him."

"Yeah. No one in the bar remembers the victim leaving. She wasn't taken by force; she left with him willingly," he reminded me.

"I think our offender is a woman."

"No way," Ben said, joining our conversation. "Women do not dole out that level of violence. They kill in the heat of passion, spur of the moment. It is rare for a woman to kill men that are not close to them."

"*Men* that are close to them. What about a woman killing women?"

"Even lower probability," Ben answered.

"Hell has no fury like a woman scorned," Mike said.

"Right. She feels inadequate, targeting women she thinks are beautiful. A bar is a hot spot for single women looking for a man. I bet the women she's targeted had men falling over themselves to talk to them that night, while she sat and watched, stewing about all her flaws and failures to get and keep a man. That's why there's no sexual assault. We profiled the offender is sexually incompetent, and in her mind, she is. The only commonality between all thirteen victims is they are pretty. Our offender defaces her victims, taking away what makes them desirable – their beauty. The single stab to the abdomen is symbolic – the womb. She cuts through the very thing she hates the most, their womanhood."

"Holy fuck," Ben said, pulling out his tablet. "I think I agree with you, Boy Wonder."

"Hey, Nick." Kristy greeted. "I ran the search for

you. I only found two women fitting your parameters. One case was solved, before you ask, iron-clad DNA evidence and the boyfriend confessed. That leaves Meadow Holiday. Here's her file."

Kristy dropped the folder and walked away before I could thank her.

"What's that?" Mike asked.

"I had Kristy run victims with a single stab wound and facial disfiguration," I answered.

"We already did that." He rolled his eyes.

"Victims that lived."

I opened the file and sucked in a breath. I knew her. Well, I didn't know her personally, but she was a regular at my favorite coffee shop, Sam's. Her hair was longer now than it was in her driver's license picture, but it was her. Long, sexy red hair, creamy pale complexion, and the most beautiful piercing green eyes.

I thought about the last time I saw her. Mike and I went in to grab a cup of coffee after an early morning basketball game, and she was sitting in her usual spot in the corner. Unapproachable, closed off to the world. Meadow Holiday did not invite conversation.

"Shit."

"What?" Ben asked, and both men looked at me.

"This." I held the photo up for them to see.

"Holy shit, is that the girl from Sam's you drool over?" Mike asked.

"I do not drool over her," I corrected.

"Then what do you call it?" he laughed.

"Admire from afar. She's standoffish and refuses to make eye contact. Sits in the same corner with her back to the wall. The first time I saw her, she didn't have the scar. It must've been a month, maybe two later, she appeared again, and the scar was there. That was about five years ago. I hadn't started the academy yet. I think I was waiting to class up."

I scanned the report, no ketamine. Damn.

"Hey, Ben. What is maprotiline?" I asked.

"A tetracyclic antidepressant. Why?"

"No ketamine in her tox report, but maprotiline was present. Goddamn." I shook my head at the image of Meadow.

"What?" Mike asked. I held up the new image for him to see.

Meadow's face had a single slash mark, from her ear down across her cheek, ending at the corner of her jaw. Her pretty face was marred with black stitches. The image ignited a blaze in my chest I'd never experienced before. I'd seen hundreds of pictures of victims, and sadly the image I was holding up was mild in comparison. Seeing her like this was different. Something clicked, and a side of myself I'd never known came to life. I wanted to find the person who'd dared to hurt her, not to put behind bars, but to beat the shit out of them, make them feel the same pain she had.

"Earth to Nick..." Mike laughed.

"What?"

"Damn. Boy Wonder is day dreaming about the pretty vic," Mike smiled.

"Don't call her that. Her name is Meadow."

Meadow.

Beautiful. Unique. Just like the woman herself. The name fit.

"Are we going to talk to her?" Mike asked.

"Yeah. I think we should visit her at her work. We'd scare the shit out of her if we showed up at her house," I suggested.

"I agree."

"I'm going to cross reference doctors prescribing both ketamine and maprotiline. I'll update Joel and Mandy. When you get back, we'll call in Kilby and fill him in." Ben said, not looking up from his tablet.

"Great. Let's go." I grabbed my cell and keys off my desk and headed for the door.

6

Nick

"MISS HOLIDAY?"

Holy sweet mother of God it was him. And if I thought he was good looking in the coffee house, I'd been wrong. He was way better than good looking. And tall. Even though I'd just seen him last week at Sam's, I'd been sitting, and I'd forgotten how much taller he was than me.

"Miss?" he asked again.

"Yes. That's me."

"I'm SA Clark and this is SA Gonzalez. Sorry to bother you at work, but is there somewhere we can speak privately?"

Both men held out badges and easily flipped the

leather wallet, flashing FBI – Special Agent credentials on the other side.

"Did something happen?" I asked.

"No, ma'am. We just need a quick word in private. If now's not a good time we can schedule a meeting in a public place. Sam's perhaps?"

Shit. He recognized me. Did he think I was stalking him?

"Can you tell me what it's about?" I asked.

"We need to ask you a few questions about your attack," the other man answered.

Attack.

My vision blurred, and I fought to keep my composure.

"Meadow?" Nick called my name. When his face came into focus, he continued, "We can do this another time. We didn't want to ambush you at work, but did think it would be best to approach you somewhere you felt safe."

Feel safe? I never felt safe. I only left my house by sheer force of will, that and after I had a dream, I had to leave, so the walls didn't close in on me.

"Did you catch him?"

"No, ma'am. We were hoping you could answer a few questions," Gonzales answered.

"Can you give me a minute to tell my boss I'm taking my lunch?"

"Certainly. Take your time." Nick smiled, only this time I didn't revel in his good looks. The fantasy of him had come to a crashing halt. He was an FBI agent and knew the details of my attack. Not that I was ever planning to talk to him, but I could pretend in my mind. Now that was over.

After a brief talk with my boss, I led the agents down the hall to the employee lounge and braced for the onslaught of misery. Both men waited for me to sit before Gonzales took the seat across the small linoleum table and Nick bought water from the vending machine and sat it in front of me.

"I'm sorry to have to ask you this, but do you remember anything new from the night you were attacked?" Nick asked.

That was the million-dollar question. The double-edged sword, so to speak. Two sides of the same blade, both equally sharp, either side would cut deep. If I could remember more, how much more devastating would my dreams be? Would I live out the whole attack in vivid detail? But by not remembering, I was of no help. The man who did this to me was still free.

"I don't understand. I was attacked five years ago. I

went through countless interviews with the police. I haven't heard from them in years."

"Again, I'm very sorry to ask you to relive something so horrible. We have a case that is similar; that's why we're here," Nick answered.

"Similar? He did it again?"

Oh no. No. No. No. I should've moved back to California when I woke up in the hospital, and my mom had begged me to move home, but I'd refused. At the time I had friends here, though they all slowly dwindled away when I didn't recover fast enough for them, and I'd continually refused to accept their invitations to go out. There was also the issue of my stepfather. He was a jerk, and I hated him. However, I should've listened to her and moved.

"Him?" Nick asked.

"What?" I asked. Now he was confusing me. Were we not talking about my attacker?

"You said him."

"Right." I drug out the word, still not understanding what he was getting at.

"What do you remember about him?" Gonzales asked.

"Nothing. I have a hazy memory of being stabbed, but the only part of that night or the attack I can clearly remember is the pain."

"The sound of the voice?" Nick asked.

"Not really. I still dream about it, but each time the voice is different. The words are always the same – but the voice changes. Sometimes I see more of the knife as it comes toward my face. Little details change, but the words never do."

Nick nudged the bottle of water and gave me a small, sad smile. He felt sorry for me, just like everyone else did. He'd be polite to me; I don't think he had it in him to look at me outright with the disgust I was sure he felt when he saw my face. Everyone did.

"What happened? Did he hurt someone again?" Neither of them had clearly explained.

"We're not sure it's the same person, and it's an ongoing investigation. I'm sorry, but I can't tell you anything about it. Would you be willing to come down to the BAU and speak to Dr. Mandy Brown? Maybe hypnosis would help bring some of the memories to the forefront," Gonzales offered.

"What makes you think I want to remember?" I snapped.

"You're right. You've been through enough. Sorry to have bothered you. I'm going to leave you my card. If you think of anything or if you need something, don't hesitate to call," Nick offered and placed a business card on the table before he stood. Gonzales followed even though he looked like he wanted to push the issue.

"Hey, Nick?" I called as they made their way to the door.

"Yeah?"

"Thanks for the water."

With a nod, they were gone.

Jesus, why was I such a freak? I didn't have to snap and bite their heads off. They were only doing their jobs. I pulled out my phone and sent Veronica Venus a message.

Me: You know... South Dakota sounds real nice right about now. Could I buy a piece of land next to yours and we can hole up like a bunch of hermits and order our food online to be delivered?

Her reply came quickly; they always did. After her attack, she started working from home.

VV21: Why? Who upset you? That bitch Beth again? When are you going to tell her to shove it up her ass?

That made me laugh. Veronica Venus knew all about my troubles with Beth and her rude comments.

Me: No. She's fine. Two detectives with the FBI just left. They had questions about my attacker. They think he attacked someone else.

VV21: WHAT? Why do they think that?

Me: IDK. They wouldn't say. It's an ongoing investigation. What if he comes after me again?

VV21: Meadow, don't go there. You're safe. Live your life. Maybe they'll catch him.

Me: Yeah, maybe. Back to work. I'll message you later.

Veronica Venus sent back a bunch of smiley faces, kisses, and a couple of cat faces.

Crazy woman. I don't know what'd I do without her.

7

Two steps ahead

ANOTHER ONE.

Always two fucking steps ahead.

"Kelley Morris, twenty-nine. Stab to the stomach, face bludgeoned with a blunt object." Joel added the new picture to the board.

Lauren Marshall, Kylie Peters, and Kelley Morris. Three young women senselessly murdered.

"Everything fits." Mandy joined Joel at the whiteboard to add the girl's DMV picture. "The media has released the story. They broke the news a little after 3 a.m., shortly after the body was found. It replayed at 6 a.m. Kilby has decided to use the coverage to his advantage and set up a hotline. The PD made a statement as well about the extra police presence, trying to settle the public's fear."

"So much for keeping it quiet," Ben mumbled.

"Yeah. You knew that wasn't going to happen as soon as the buzzards caught a sniff," Joel huffed.

The public was going to be in a panic, and there were going to be thousands of well-meaning citizens calling in with information, stretching the PD's already thin resources.

It was barely coming up on 9 a.m. and my day had already gone to hell in a handbasket.

My phone vibrated, an unknown number flashing on the screen.

"SA Clark," I answered.

"Hi. Um. This is Meadow Holiday. Is this Nick?"

"Hi, Meadow. Are you okay?"

She sounded like she'd been crying and her voice was shaky and unsure.

"I didn't know where else to go."

"Go? Where are you? Are you safe? Stay put. I'll come to you."

I was already out the doors of the BAU heading to the lobby when I felt Mike at my back.

"I'm here. Well, at the address on your card. I'm sorry to bother you."

"Here? In the parking lot?"

We made it to the front of the building, and I scanned the area for Meadow, but I didn't see her.

"I'm in my car. I'm too afraid to get out," she cried.

My heart pounded in my chest, and an unexplainable fury pulsed through my veins. She was scared to death. That pissed me off enough, but if one hair on her head was hurt, I'd lose my ever-loving mind.

"There." Mike pointed to a white Honda Accord. Sure enough, Meadow was in the driver's seat, her forehead on the steering wheel.

"You did the right thing staying in your car. I want you to look out your window. Mike and I are walking toward your car now." I watched as she lifted her head, looking toward the building. "Do you see us?"

"Yeah."

"I don't want to scare you more than you are. Mike has his weapon drawn; it is for our safety. He won't hurt you."

"I see you," she sobbed.

A few more strides and we were at her car. I disconnected and shoved my phone in my back pocket and opened the car door, not bothering to check the area before I pulled Meadow out and into my arms. I knew Mike would cover me while I took care of Meadow. I scanned her from top to toe, no blood or visible injury. Thank God.

"What do you need from your car?" I asked.

"Keys."

I reached in, pulled them from the ignition, slammed the door, beeped her locks, and gave Mike a chin lift. Without a word, Meadow allowed me to guide her into the lobby, down the corridor, and into the BAU office.

When we entered Mike broke away, going to his desk to give us privacy.

"Are you okay? Did someone try and hurt you?"

I was going out of my mind not knowing what'd scared her bad enough to drive to the FBI office listed on my business card. She didn't even know if I was there.

"I saw it," she cried.

"Saw what?" I walked her a few more feet to the closest desk and sat her down in the chair. I knelt in front of her and asked again, "Did someone hurt you?"

"No. I'm not hurt." Thank God. "I saw the news. Is that why you came to see me? You think he did that too?"

Fuck.

Goddamned news media.

There was only so much I could tell her, but I had to be honest.

"Yes. That's why we came to see you."

"Ohmygod! Is he going to do that to me? She didn't have a face left. The news said she didn't have a face! Nick! He's gonna do that to me."

Christ Almighty.

"Hell no!" Meadow blinked and brought her gorgeous green eyes to mine, more tears spilling out of the corners. "No one is going to hurt you. We're not sure if your case is related, there are a few details that we haven't disclosed to the public that are different."

"I would've looked like that girl if the waitress hadn't heard me screaming when she went out back to throw away the trash. I know it."

I'd read Meadow's file, and I wouldn't tell her, but I agreed. The waitress had saved her life. Unfortunately, or fortunately for the waitress, she was smart and didn't run in the alley to help Meadow. She'd stood by the back door and yelled into the bar for the kitchen staff to come and help her. She was right to not rush out by herself, but the person who hurt Meadow got away unseen.

"We don't know that, and we don't know if they're related."

"I was attacked on the seventh," she sobbed.

I knew she was. The team and I firmly believed that Meadow Holiday was supposed to be victim number one.

I waited for her to slowly come back to herself and asked, "There were eleven victims who were attacked on the seventh, and I'm not accusing you of anything but did you not hear about the murders on the news?"

"No. After the... you know... I checked out. Emotionally, I mean. I could barely function through the day at work; I'd been moved from my position in sales to a file clerk. I was in the back of the office alone all day. No one spoke to me because they were all afraid I'd have a break down or something, and I had this huge scar on my face. No one wants to see that. It's gross. So, they put me where no one would have to look at me. When I got home, I'd either sit and try and remember what happened or I'd go online to my survivor message board. Sometimes I'd read, but I never watched TV. I still don't. The news is scary; TV is full of violence, and truthfully once you've lived it, you don't want to watch it. Besides, whenever I see the beautiful actresses, it just reminds me of everything I'm not."

I closed my eyes and shook my head; there was so much I wanted to say, none of it appropriate for me to say to a victim. Who had allowed this beautiful woman to suffer alone in silence? No one stood by her to pull her up and dust her off and remind her of her worth. It was a damn shame.

"First, you are beautiful." I stopped to touch the side of her face, a feather-light trace of her scar. I shouldn't have said that, and I really should not be touching her. But fuck it – in for a penny, in for a pound. "This doesn't make you any less so. You are strong, and I don't care how long it took you, you did it. You pulled yourself together and survived. I'm sorry this is happening, but I'll make sure you're safe."

Another line I shouldn't have crossed. Never promise something you can't deliver. We've yet to catch the offender - fourteen dead women, and still nothing.

"I'll talk to that Dr. Mandy, sorry I forgot her last name, if you think it will help."

So fucking brave. She reminded me of my Aunt Reagan in that regard. When I was eleven and first went to live with my Uncle Nolan, Reagan had been kidnapped and held on an abandoned oil rig. The man that took her was using the rig as a makeshift hospital to harvest black market organs. Before my uncle could get to her, one of Reagan's kidneys was removed and sold. My aunt pushed through her pain to make sure everyone around her was okay. My family tried to shield me from as much of the details as they could, but that experience was a defining moment in my life. Right before my eyes, I watched as my family came together to rally around my aunt. Family was everything.

I didn't think Meadow had that, yet she was still strong, willing to try and remember to help someone else.

"Mandy Brown. I want you to take some time and think about it. Don't make a knee-jerk decision because of what you saw on the news. Hypnosis doesn't always work, but if it does, you will remember things that your mind has buried."

"It wasn't only the news. I've been thinking about it the last few days. I was going to call you; I was working up the nerve. When I saw the news, I panicked. I'm sorry I came here, but I couldn't think of anything else to do."

"I'm glad you did. I told you if you needed anything to call," I reminded her.

"Yeah, but when you said that, I don't think you meant from the parking lot in a middle of a psychotic break."

"Red, I've seen psychotic breaks, and that wasn't one. When I told you to call me, I meant from anywhere, anytime. You did the right thing. Let me get you something to drink, and I'll see where Mandy is and introduce you. Sorry, we don't have Sam's vanilla coffee here. You're stuck with water, bureau coffee, or I'm sure I can find you a soda if you'd like one."

Her pretty, creamy skin tinted pink and she smiled. "How'd you know I like vanilla coffee?"

"Probably the same way you knew my name was Nick."

"What do you mean, you told me your name."

"No, Red, I introduced myself as SA Clark. And I did show you my credentials, but I always cover my name with my finger when I flip my shield. I don't like the public knowing my full name."

Her blush deepened, and she cracked a smile. "Okay. You totally caught me. I knew your name from Sam's, but I didn't want you to think I was a stalker or something. I'm not. It was the first day, and we were standing next to each other. Becky called out Nick, and you reached for the coffee, so I kinda knew from that."

She was so damn cute when she forgot to be scared and wasn't hiding her face.

"Same way I knew what kind of coffee you liked. So? What will it be?"

"How bad is the bureau coffee?"

I was so happy to see the smile hadn't left her face and even happier that I put it there.

"Palatable, barely."

"Coffee, please."

"Coming right up. I'll be back."

I found Mandy and the rest of the guys in the conference room. Thankfully they'd drawn the blinds on the only window that looked out into the main area of the office. The last thing Meadow needed to see was pictures of thirteen dead women. I caught everyone up on Meadow's willingness to try hypnosis. Everyone nodded their approval and Mandy followed me to meet Meadow.

I made a quick introduction, gave Meadow her coffee, and left them talking. I thought she'd feel more comfortable speaking with Mandy alone. Now I wasn't so sure. Every few minutes I'd look up and catch Meadow giving me sidelong glances, but when I tried to hold her stare, she'd look away.

Damn Nick. Get a grip.

I had a bad case of wishful thinking.

8

Sally

"TAKE a few days and think about it. I'd like you to read the information I gave you on hypnosis." Dr. Mandy Brown had a calming grandmotherly appeal, though I didn't think she'd appreciate me thinking of her as grandmotherly; she looked younger than my mom.

"Thank you for not thinking I'm crazy," I told her.

"Why would I think you're crazy?"

"For starters, I drove here in a complete freak out because I saw the news and had convinced myself someone was watching me then..."

"Wait. You thought someone was watching you?

What do you mean?" Her posture suddenly changed, and her smile disappeared.

"See? Crazy. I get the feeling a lot. When I talk to my friend who is also a survivor of a violent attack, she says it's normal, that I'll always feel that way and I should ignore it."

Veronica Venus has been my rock over the last few years. I would've become the hermit I'd joked with her about becoming if it wasn't for her talking me off the ledge. The first month I went back to work was the worst. Every time I stepped foot into the office, I could swear someone was staring at me. When I broke down and talked to Veronica Venus about it, she laughed and said, *of course they are.* It took some getting used to, everyone staring at me and watching me. After a while, I was able to push it back and ignore it. I still get the creeps sometimes, and all the hair on my arms will stand up reminding me that I'm a freak.

"Tell me about this time. Where were you? What were you doing?" Mandy asked.

"It really is my imagination. I was getting ready for work. I clicked on the TV to check the weather and news about the girl that was found last night was on. When the broadcast showed the alley, I dropped my coffee. All I could think about was I was found in an alley. That could've been me. No one was watching me; it's all in my head. I know it, but it's like there's this disconnect between my brain and my body's reaction. I can't explain it."

"I think you explained it just fine. Where were you in your house?"

I was sorry I'd brought up my silly notions about imaginary people watching me. It was nothing, something I'd learned to live with.

"I was in my living room – alone. Safe and sound; the only threat to my well-being is my overactive crazy thoughts."

She seemed to contemplate what I'd said and thankfully dropped it.

"I think you did the right thing coming here. It is always better to be safe than sorry. You have my numbers. Use them if you need to, day or night. And please, Meadow, if you ever think you're in danger – drive here immediately. The lobby of this building never closes."

"Thank you. But that won't be necessary. I know you can't tell me anything. Nick explained the case is ongoing, but do you think the same guy that attacked me killed all those women?"

That was the question I needed answered the most.

"I think there's a strong possibility." Mandy didn't bother to sugar coat the news, which I appreciated.

"Do you think you can hypnotize me?" I tried to fight back the tears, but when one rolled down my cheek, I angrily swiped it away. I'd given this asshole too many tears. Too many sleepless nights. Too much!

"Yes. But I still want you to think about it."

"Okay." After all this time, of trying my hardest to forget that night, it was time to dig deep and push through the pain of the memories. If my suffering could save one woman's life, then it would be worth it. "Thank you for taking the time to explain everything to me. I'll think about it tonight and call you tomorrow."

"You're very welcome. Would you like to talk to Nick before you leave?" she asked, and I felt my cheeks heat.

I didn't want her to think I was some kook who was stalking her partner or making stuff up to get close to him.

"That's alright. I don't want to bother him," I said regretfully, even though I wanted nothing more than to see him one more time.

"Don't be silly. He'll want to see you're okay before you leave anyway." She smiled.

We found Nick across the room, not that I hadn't been tracking his movements around the room the entire time Mandy had been speaking to me. I couldn't help it; my eyes had always been drawn to him. Even in the busy coffee house I could look through the crowd and zero in on him immediately. But now that the deep rumble of his voice had been directed at me, it seemed whatever weird connection I'd felt had locked into place, and I couldn't stop looking to him for comfort. Just knowing he was close made my body tingle and come alive, a feeling I hadn't had for a very long time. More than that, he made me want to be brave. I had to know something that would help them catch the man that was killing these women. Hopefully, Mandy could unlock the memories I'd worked hard to bury deep in my mind, in a vault with double padlocks where I could never access them.

"Everything okay?" Nick asked when we approached.

"Yeah." Mandy laughed. "Meadow is getting ready to leave."

Nick's features softened when his gaze landed on me. "I'll walk you to your car," he offered.

"Oh no. I've taken up enough of your time. I don't want to bother you."

Now that I'd calmed down, I was embarrassed I'd rushed over here and made a fool of myself, crying in my car like a complete freak.

"No bother. Besides, I was leaving anyway," he told me, pushing away from the desk he'd been leaning against.

"Going to pick up Sally?" Mr. Gonzales asked.

"Yeah. Lazy girl was still sleeping when I left." He smiled at the other agent. "I'll be back in thirty minutes."

Shit. I was so stupid. Of course, someone as good looking as Nick Clark would have a girlfriend or wife. Damn, I was a total bitch lusting after another woman's man. Not that I'd ever thought he'd give me a second glance. Not only was my face hideous but I had nothing to offer a man. I'd help the FBI as much as I could, then I'd slink away and go back to my pitiful, lonely existence, where my only source of friendship and human interaction took place over the internet.

I continued to mentally berate myself all the way to my car. Nick was quiet and watchful and waited for me to unlock and open my door before he spoke.

"Are you okay?"

"Other than being mortified at being a drama queen and having a panic attack, which led me here, where you got to witness me freaking out and crying? Yeah. I'm fine. I'll call Mandy tomorrow, and we'll set up a time for her to try and hypnotize me. Hopefully, I can remember something helpful."

Nick took a step closer, closing the already small space between us.

"Red, I'm happy you came here. You are not a drama queen. Whether you remember details that are helpful to our case is not what's important. Maybe it will help you put what happened behind you."

I stiffened at his closeness. I could feel his warm breath on my face as he spoke. Too close. Nowhere to go. No way to escape. I was trapped between his hard body and the door jamb.

"Whoa, Meadow. I'm sorry. I didn't mean to scare you."

"It's umm... it's fine. I'm fine. I'll let you get on with your day. Thanks again for all your help."

I maneuvered into the driver's seat and quickly shut the door. I knew it was rude, and I'd cut him off as he'd begun to speak, but I couldn't bear to stand next to him a second longer.

It hurt.

I physically ached from the closeness.

He was everything I could no longer have.

9

Marriage?

WHAT THE FUCK HAPPENED?

I'd asked myself that question a thousand times over the last twenty-four hours. I'd never read a woman so wrong in all my life. I'd convinced myself that Meadow felt the same attraction I did when clearly that was not the case. She couldn't have fled faster if she grew wings and took flight. The woman didn't even want to stand close to me.

Damn shame!

I couldn't shake the feeling, even knowing she didn't feel the same insane pull I did. The emotion had taken root and the harder I tried to stop thinking about her, the more I did. The way her pretty, green eyes had sparkled with tears, the way she'd searched me out across the room, even the way she pulled her hair over her left shoulder trying to hide the scar on her face was endearing.

I. Couldn't. Stop. Or maybe I didn't want to. I'd never had such an instant and strong connection with a woman, especially a woman I barely knew. There was something about Meadow Holiday that checked all the boxes.

"Settle."

At my command, Sally stopped her overeager puppy bounce and stood at my side. The order in no way stopped her excitement of being at the office. Her tail was wagging with such force her rear-end was moving in sync.

"I'm impressed. A month ago she would've completely ignored you and run around the office looking for something to chew," Mike said.

"How much longer do you have her?" Mandy asked.

"She was supposed to go to Gabe next month, but he has another surgery scheduled. So, it's up in the air. Alexandra wants him fully healed before he takes her," I explained.

First Class Petty Officer Gabe Lavine had been matched with Sally by Homefront, an organization that pairs comfort animals with vets. Sally was the fourth dog I'd fostered and trained for the charity. Alexandra was meticulous about pairing the right owner with the right dog. When the shepherd was matched for Gabe, she was given to me to train.

"I'm gonna miss her coming in with you," Mike said and bent down to give Sally a scratch.

"Me too. It's gonna suck when she leaves."

Mandy's desk phone rang, and she broke away to answer, leaving Mike and me with Sally.

"You're totally transparent," he laughed.

"What do you mean?"

"Meadow's coming in today," he told me, something I already knew.

"And?" I prompted.

"And? You happened to bring in Sally."

So, Mike had seen right through my plan. One thing my uncles taught me was to improvise. Sally was a great ice breaker, and I was hoping to use her to draw Meadow out. I admit using a dog to get close to Meadow was a tad underhanded, but all is fair in love and war, right? Not that this was love so much as it was white-hot attraction and interest, but the same rules applied.

It was not beneath me to do whatever it took to get Meadow's attention.

"I have no idea what you're talking about." I smiled at Mike before I turned to Sally and gestured her to *come.* "Good girl," I praised when she followed me to my desk and laid on the floor at my feet.

For the next three hours Mike, Joel and I combed over all the information we had on *The Butcher.* Fourteen dots on a map marked where the bodies had been found. The killer had remained inside a thirty-mile comfort zone. While that narrowed it down, there were still hundreds of bars in the area. Hundreds of locations the killer could strike.

"Jesus Christ. We're on the clock with less than a month until we find another body. I hope to God Meadow Holiday can remember something useful," Mike muttered.

"We narrowed it down to five doctors prescribing both ketamine and maprotiline," Joel said, adding, "Ben is following up with them to get their patient lists. With HIPAA the way it is, it would've been faster for Kristy to get us the information, but Kilby wanted it by the book. Which means time, time we don't fucking have."

"I've been thinking about the security feeds." I started, but Mike interrupted me.

"Hold that thought. Meadow's here."

I looked out the conference room window, and

there she was. Goddamn, she was beautiful. She looked too small standing next to Mandy. And it had nothing to do with her height. Mandy stood tall and confident, while Meadow folded into herself, trying to disappear. That wouldn't do! There was no reason for a woman so stunning and sweet to be hiding the way Meadow was.

"Close the blinds," Joel said, as he stacked the police reports scattered about the table.

Mike closed the blinds, and I turned the whiteboards around so the images of the dead girls faced the wall. Mandy would be bringing Meadow in here, and the last thing she needed to see before being hypnotized was a bunch of women with their faces mutilated and mangled.

Sally continued to sit as the women entered the room, her ears had perked up and her body was vibrating with excitement but she hadn't otherwise moved.

"Meadow, you remember the guys, right?" Mandy asked.

"Oh my gosh. She's beautiful. I love shepherds," Meadow said, ignoring Mandy's question. I mentally high fived myself and glanced over at Mike just in time to see him roll his eyes. "May I pet her?"

"Sure. Sally, up." Sally stood, and the butt wagging

was so intense her tail was making a swooshing sound. "Gentle." I gave Sally the all clear, and she took off, her nails scraping the laminate floor as she skidded to a stop in front of Meadow and sat.

"Sally?" Meadow asked, and Sally looked up at her, tongue lolling out and all but drooling. I hoped to God she didn't jump on Meadow and lick her face. That had been the first habit we broke, but as well trained as she was, she was a puppy. And she was excited to meet a new friend. "Her name is Sally?"

"Yeah." I wasn't sure where she was going with the question. But suddenly I felt self-conscious about the dog having a human name. "I didn't name her, Alexandra did." I felt the need to explain, but when Meadow's face fell, I regretted trying.

"Well, if you ladies are ready, we'll get out of your way." Mike grabbed the folders off the table and headed for the door, Joel right behind him.

I still hadn't moved. I was overly concerned with Meadow and her interest in Sally's name.

"What's wrong?" I asked.

"Nothing. Umm... why?" She was lying.

"Mandy, can you give us a minute?" I wasn't sure why I felt the need to understand why Meadow's expression had changed, and why she suddenly seemed... sad, but I did, and I was going to find out.

Mandy left the room and clicked the door closed behind her. Meadow continued to rub Sally's ears and refused to look at me.

"What just happened?" I asked again.

"What do you mean?"

"Well, you walked in here smiling, and now you look like someone told you Santa wasn't real."

"You and your wife have a beautiful dog. I've always wanted a shepherd."

"My wife?"

What the hell was she talking about?

"Oh, I'm sorry. Your girlfriend."

"My girlfriend?"

The light was beginning to dawn.

"Alexandra?"

There it was. She thought I had a woman. So, I hadn't imagined the attraction. I smiled at the realization and thought back to when she turned from looking toward me with something that looked a lot like longing to icy. It was after I said I was going to check on Sally. The girl was confused.

"Alexandra owns an organization called Home-front. They match vets with dogs. I volunteer there, fostering dogs until their permanent home is ready and the dog is trained to meet their needs. Sally belongs to a vet named Gabe," I explained.

"Oh. Ummm. I thought..." she trailed off, not finishing her thought.

"That I had a woman," I finished for her.

"Yeah."

Her cheeks pinkened, and I wanted to fist bump the air.

"Are you ready for today?" I asked and noticed she hadn't stopped petting Sally. Good. I'd leave her in here with Meadow when her and Mandy had their session.

"I think so. I barely slept last night. I worried I won't remember now that I want to. I've spent so much time pushing the memories away. It will be my luck I did a good job, and Mandy won't be able to find them."

"You'll do fine. All you need to do is relax. Mandy is great; she'll stop whenever you need her to. Don't push it. If it gets to be too much, you can try again, or not."

"I want to do this. If somewhere locked inside of me is the break you need to find this guy, I want to remember. I don't want anyone else to die."

She kept saying man, guy, him. I wondered if those pronouns were an assumption or if she knew it was a man. I still hadn't asked, that was for Mandy to dig through. I didn't want to put any ideas in her head.

"So damn brave," I told her.

"What? I'm not brave. I hide away from everyone."

She looked so sad and was folding into herself again. That shit had to stop. If I did nothing else, I'd make sure when this was over Meadow Holiday stood tall and proud.

"Red, you don't give yourself enough credit. Most people, after what you went through, don't recover. You have. You are brave and sweet, and so damn pretty. You're breaking my heart standing there hunched over. You don't have one damn thing to hide. And before you say it, or point it out, the scar on your face doesn't do a goddamn thing to take away from how beautiful you are."

It was painful to watch her recoil at my words.

"There's nothing beautiful about me. Not anymore. Trust me. I'm better off blending in and being a loner. I have nothing to offer anyone."

I was wrong. Listening to her wasn't painful, it was pure agony. My gut twisted hearing her say she had nothing to offer. As much as I wanted to correct her and tell her. she had everything, she was everything, it wasn't the right time. She needed to be relaxed and not freaked out when I turned into a caveman and beat my chest until she understood just how lovely she was.

"Red, you have no idea what you're talking about." Before she could protest, I asked, "Do you want me to leave Sally in here with you while you talk to Mandy? She seems to like you."

"I think I'd like that if it's okay."

"Sure, it is. Mandy knows her commands, and if she starts to misbehave, I'll come in and get her."

Suddenly I was unsure about Meadow being hypnotized. What if she did remember and it set her back? Mandy knocked on the door at the same time as she opened it poking her head in.

"You ready?" she asked.

"As I'll ever be." Meadow tried to smile, but it didn't reach her eyes. Hell, it barely pulled the corner of her mouth up.

Fuck. I didn't like this, but it wasn't my place to stop her. And truth be told we needed a break, some bit of information that would help us catch this asshole.

"I'll be right outside."

Before I could change my mind, I left the conference room and walked right into Joel.

"Damn, boy, you've got it bad." He chuckled.

"What are you talking about?"

On an exhale he shook his head as if he was irritated, but the smile told me he was anything but. "I'm changing your name. You've been upgraded from Boy Wonder to Glass. You're in a room full of men that not only are trained to crawl into your head and extrapolate any and every emotion, but we are *men*. Dude, we see right through you. You're not hiding shit. From the moment that woman entered the building, you've been hovering. Shit bro, I think we have some bubble wrap in the supply closet if you'd like to wrap her up."

I thought about lying and telling Joel he was full of shit, but he was right, I was hovering. And I wasn't doing a damn thing to hide it.

"I can't explain it. I don't know why she's different. And before you say it, it has nothing to do with her being a victim. I don't have a savior complex. I've watched her for years at the coffee house. I was going to try and talk to her, but one day she was there, then she was gone for a long time. When she started going to the shop again, she was a different person. Not one part of her hinted she was approachable. She'd made an effort to avoid everyone. So I left her alone. Big mistake."

"You've got your work cut out for you." He made a low whistling sound. "Hope you're ready for her."

"What does that mean?" I asked.

"You'll find out soon enough. I've been married a long time. It took me two years to ask my wife out on our first date."

"Okay." That was interesting and all, but I didn't

see what Joel's courting process with his wife had to do with this or the insane attraction I felt toward Meadow.

"It took me two years to get my shit straight. I knew the minute, the very second, I'd clapped eyes on my Ellie, she was mine. I knew I was going to marry her. So, I waited until I was ready to be the man she needed before I asked her on our first date." Joel didn't wait for my response, with a slap to my shoulder he moved to his desk and sat down as if he hadn't just rocked my world.

Marriage?

No one said anything about marriage. I was infatuated with the woman, I couldn't stop thinking about her, and sure I wanted to know everything about her. Hell, I was still on the fence about asking her out.

Marriage? Crazy old man.

10

Assumptions

"YOU'RE DOING GREAT."

Mandy had turned off most of the overhead lights, leaving only a small amount of light, and with the door closed it was surprisingly quiet in the room.

"Have you ever been hypnotized before?" she asked.

"No," I answered and continued to concentrate on rubbing Sally's head like she'd told me to do.

"It's not like what you see on TV. You won't fall asleep or even be sleepy. Hypnosis is a state of focused relaxation. It's simply a psychological state, a different kind of awareness, where your brain will be more open to memories. Your focus will change from perceived expectations to the actual event." Mandy's voice was soft and soothing as she spoke. "I want you to continue to pet Sally. Relax and only think about how soft her fur is. Good. It's soft and smooth. Now slow your breathing - deep, slow breaths, good."

Mandy's voice gentled as she spoke, and it was becoming difficult to concentrate on her words. The sound alone was calming. Sally's head had long ago rested on my lap; it was heavy and warm, anchoring me to the chair I was sitting in.

"Keeping your eyes closed, I want you to tell me what you had for dinner last night."

"Orange chicken and white rice."

"Meadow, what did you have to drink with your orange chicken and white rice?"

"A Diet Coke out of a can."

"Tell me what you were drinking at the Blue Bird."

"Gin and soda."

"Did you have lime or lemon with your gin?"

I thought back to that night. I had to wait to get the bartender's attention. When I finally did, I ordered gin and soda. The noise level was so loud I had to yell over the bar for extra lemon.

"Extra lemon."

"Where were you when you ordered your drink?"

"At the bar."

"Tell me about that night. You ordered your drink, what happened next?"

"The bar was packed. Wall-to-wall people. I picked up my drink and headed to a table that a waitress was clearing. I sat down and checked my phone. My friend Maya was late, and I hated being there by myself. I sipped on my drink, and after a few more minutes I checked my phone again. I had a missed text message. Maya had a fender bender and was tied up with the accident and had to cancel. There were so many people looking for an open table I felt bad and went back to the bar so someone else could use the table. I finished my drink, and I ordered another. I was talking to someone."

"Who were you talking to?"

"I don't know. They're right there at the bar, but I can't see."

"Okay. Skip it. Can you remember what you were talking about?"

"Purses. The bartender had filled a beer glass too full, and some had spilled when he was passing it to a patron, and it got on her purse. It was expensive. She called the bartender a clumsy idiot. I was horribly embarrassed at how rude she was. I wanted to leave, but then she apologized to the man, and I felt better. So, I stayed."

"What kind of purse was it?"

"It was a four-hundred-dollar Coach Edie Shoulder bag. She told me it was a gift from her boyfriend. I thought it looked like a waste of money."

"You're sitting at the bar talking about purses. What happened next?"

"She was telling me the purse was a gift. The only nice thing her boyfriend ever gave her. I was bumped from behind and spilled some of my drink on my shirt. I looked behind me, and someone had fallen. I got up and helped the drunk girl to her feet. Her friends apologized for her bumping into my stool, and I sat back down and finished my drink."

"What else did you and the woman talk about other than purses."

"She was flirting with the bartender, but he wasn't paying attention to her. I couldn't understand why she was hitting on the man when she had a boyfriend. I wasn't feeling well. I'd only had two drinks, but I thought I was going to be sick. She helped me up and took me past the line to get into the restroom out the back door, so I could throw up. My head felt fuzzy, and if she wasn't holding me up, I wouldn't be able to walk."

"Where are you?"

"In an alley. We walked out the emergency exit. The door was propped open."

"Did you throw up?"

"No. I thought I was going to, but the fresh air felt good. I was so hot inside the bar."

"Where is the woman now?"

"She's yelling at me. I tried to cover my ears, but I can't get my arms to work. My head is pounding. She won't stop screaming at me. Over and over. My head is going to explode. It hurts."

"Focus on her words."

"She's really mad. So mad. I don't want her yelling at me."

"Focus on only the words. Not the pain or anger. What is she saying?"

"She called me a bitch and a thief and pushed me on the ground. I landed on my hands and knees but couldn't hold myself up. I rolled onto my back, and she was standing over me."

"Tell me what she's saying."

"I don't know. Her lips are moving, but she is fuzzy. I can see her but I can't. I know she's talking."

"Okay, skip it. Relax into the moment. What are you doing?"

"I'm begging. *Please don't do this.* She kneeled beside me and said, *you think because you're so pretty you can have whatever you want. Take and take. Steal what doesn't belong to you."*

"Good. What do you see?"

"She has a big kitchen knife. She raised it back to her shoulder. I told her I didn't steal anything. I begged her not to hurt me."

"What hand was holding the knife?"

"Right hand."

"Look at her hand. Focus on her fingers and tell me exactly what you see."

"I don't know. It's too hazy, and I can't see clearly."

"Does she have light skin or dark skin?"

"Light."

"Good. What happens next?"

"Pain. Pain everywhere. I feel every inch the knife is pushed into my stomach. Everything hurts. It's too much. I want it to stop. I can't make it stop. I'm hot, and I can't breathe."

"Skip it, Meadow. There is no more pain. What is she saying to you?"

"You shouldn't take what isn't yours, you dirty bitch."

"Then what do you see?"

"Nothing. My head is pounding, and I can't see anything. I can hear her breathing heavy. I can't see her. She's right there. Right in my face. She is right there!"

"Meadow! That's enough. Open your eyes and look at me."

"She's there, right there looking at me. I can feel her. Why can't I see her? The image is so close; I want to see her."

"That. Is. Enough." Mandy clapped her hands in front of my face, and I opened my eyes.

Unlike what I'd seen in movies when someone is hypnotized, and they wake up not knowing what'd happened – I could remember everything I'd told Mandy.

"Take a breath and relax. Let the image go."

"I can almost see it, Mandy."

"It doesn't matter. You did great. Give your mind a rest. The harder you try to force yourself to see it, the fuzzier it will become. Leave it."

She was right. The more I tried, the less I could see.

"A woman attacked me." I had never taken into consideration it had been a woman who had hurt me. All these years I'd assumed it was a man, refusing to remember anything but a few sentences from that night. "When I dream about what happened in the alley, I hear her yelling at me. But the voice is never the same. Sometimes it's high-pitched and shrill, and other times it's almost robotic. Same words, different voices."

"Is the voice always a woman's voice?"

"No. Male and female both. I always thought it was a man."

"The mind is programmed to process information in the way we perceive it. That's why I wanted to try to hypnotize you. All that happened was we removed the expectation and your mind was free to remember."

Holy shit. All these years I'd thought a man had tried to kill me. I wasn't sure how to feel about the new revelation. A woman!

11

Red

THAT EASILY HAD to have been the worst hour of my life. Hearing a victim relive an attack is always hard, but Meadow? It took every ounce of self-control I had not to barge into the conference room and scoop her up into my arms and hold her. I hated she was having to remember. I couldn't bear to hear her pain as she relived the attack.

"Damn, that was rough," Ben said. He'd gotten to the office in time to watch Mandy's session with Meadow.

"Seems Nick was correct. We're dealing with a female offender. I'll admit, I had my doubts but damn if he wasn't right." Joel looked up from his tablet. "I forwarded the session to Kilby. He'll be back in an hour. He wants to sit down to revise the profile. Officer Lance is coming in with him."

One step closer. Meadow's pain wasn't in vain. We were one step closer. Hopefully, the police could make an arrest before the twentieth.

"How is she?" I asked Mandy when she joined us.

"She's... okay. She actually would like to talk to you before she leaves."

I didn't bother answering Mandy. I hadn't realized how tense I had been until she told me that Meadow wanted to see me. I didn't know why, but the thought of Meadow leaving without saying goodbye sat in my gut like a rock.

Meadow sat slumped forward in the chair, scratching Sally's ears. Seeing her with Sally made me want to talk to Alexandra about getting a dog for Meadow. Homefront usually only paired comfort animals with vets, but if anyone ever needed one of their dogs, it was Meadow.

"Hey."

"Hi. Thanks for letting me borrow Sally. She's a really good dog, you've done a great job with her."

"Thanks. I'm gonna be sad when she has to go. But then, I always am. I'm glad she helped."

"Did...umm... you watch too?"

"I did. Mandy explained that the session was going to be recorded, right?" Meadow's face drained of all color, and she immediately looked away from me. "Hey. Don't do that. You have nothing to be ashamed of. You did great. I know how difficult that was for you. How are you feeling?"

"Foolish. I can't believe I blocked out a woman had attacked me. Did you know?"

"No. Only recently, when the case reopened, did we consider the unsub could be a woman. However, it wasn't until you confirmed it that we knew for sure."

"How did you figure out I was the first... you know," she asked.

"I ran a search for women who had similar wounds to the victims, crossing that with assaults that took place on the seventh."

"Why didn't she kill me?"

Meadow's tears were my undoing. I couldn't stand to see them fall down her pretty cheeks.

"Sally, up." When Sally stood I knelt in front of Meadow, grabbing her hands in mine, I squeezed until she lifted her eyes to mine. "She was interrupted by one of the bar staff."

"Some days I wish..."

"Don't say it," I interrupted. "Don't even think it.

We're gonna catch her, Red, and she's gonna pay for what she did to you."

"I better get to work. I only took half a day off."

Work? Was she crazy? She needed to go home and relax.

"Any way you can take the rest of the day?" I asked.

"No. I'm hourly. If I want to continue to buy five-dollar coffees and pay my rent I need the hours."

That was going to change. In the very near future, she wouldn't have to worry about her five-dollar coffees; I'd be buying them for her.

"What time are you done with work?" I asked.

"Five."

"Perfect. How about I pick you up at five-thirty and we go grab some dinner?"

If her cheeks had not been stained with tears, I might've laughed at how wide her green eyes got before she squinted and shook her head.

"What? Why?"

"I could tell you that I want to take you to dinner because I want to make sure you are okay. But that'd mostly be a lie."

"So, you don't care if I'm okay?" Her lip twitched, and I was relieved.

"I'm quite sure you'll be more than okay after dinner."

"What makes you think I want to have dinner with you?" Fuck. I overplayed my hand. "I'm kidding." And for the first time since I'd met her, Meadow Holiday graced me with a smile. A real one that hit her eyes and made the green shine.

Goddamn, she was beautiful.

"All joking aside. I'm fine. You don't have to waste your night having dinner with me."

"Red, not a moment would be wasted; I get to spend time with you."

I hoped the poor girl didn't play poker; she couldn't hide a single expression.

"Okay. Dinner would be nice."

———

BY THE TIME Officer Lance and Kilby made their way to the office, it was a quarter to four. Meadow lived at least thirty minutes away, and I still had to take Sally home before I picked her up. Of all fucking days to be running late.

The men watched Mandy's session with Meadow, and I wanted to crawl out of my skin. Watching the first time had been bad enough, but the second time was torture.

"Dr. Brown, can you walk me through your interview?" Officer Lance asked. The skepticism was hard to miss.

"I see you're not a believer." Mandy smiled at the man. "As you saw on the recording, I explained to Meadow hypnosis is a psychological state of focused relaxation - an altered state of awareness where your mental process works differently. It's called top-down processing. The brain processes top-level information first – memories and expectations. Those memories have a big impact on the bottom – and how your brain senses or perceives those expectations. When Meadow relaxed and focused on the details of her attack while she was in an altered state, she was able to remember what she saw, felt, and heard, not what she thought she was supposed to see.

"Top-down processing explains the placebo effect. A doctor gives a patient a pill, real or fake, and tells him he'll feel great after he takes it. He feels better. His brain expects it. He has an involuntary reaction to the pill," Mandy finished.

"Hypnosis opens your mind to suggestion," Officer Lance countered.

"Of course, it can. But as you saw, I didn't offer suggestions."

"I'm not sure I'm sold on the woman serial killer. Women don't kill with such extreme aggression."

"They don't, or they can't?" I asked.

"What do you mean, SA Clark?"

"You said they don't kill with such extreme aggression. That's not true. Women kill with the same brutality as a man. However, they typically don't become serial, but that doesn't mean they can't."

"What makes this woman different? If we had fourteen dead men on our hands, I might be apt to believe a woman was the offender," the officer continued.

"When a woman is wronged, say her husband or boyfriend cheats on her, she blames the woman. It's the woman's fault her man stepped out of the relationship. What does *she* have that I don't? Why her? Women obsess; they fixate on what they think are their own inadequacies. It consumes them and eats at their self-worth until they turn vengeful and indignant. The offender cannot kill the object of her obsession, so she kills substitutes, beautiful women that remind her of all the things she is not. She defaces her victims, taking their beauty and turning it into something unattractive and grotesque," Mandy explained.

"Why the stab to the stomach?" Officer Lance's tone had turned slightly less argumentative. "The overkill to the face is enough to kill them.

"Symbolic. The trauma is always to the lower abdomen, pelvic region," Ben answered.

"Goddamn. That's one pissed off woman," the officer agreed. "Why the change in dates?"

"Trauma. The first trigger happened on the seventh. Four years later a second trigger happened on the twentieth," Joel told him.

"It's no secret I don't put a lot of stock into profiling. It's a crapshoot. But we can use all the help we can get, so I'd appreciate a new report I can present to my guys. We already have more patrols set for the twentieth, but I can't cover every bar in the city. My tech specialist has tried to recover the last crime scene's security hard drive with no luck. I've asked SSA Kilby to let your girl take a crack at it. I hope we catch this bitch before I have another dead woman with her face mutilated."

"We'll have something for you in the morning, and Kristy is already working on the hard drive." Kilby stood, signaling the meet was over. The rest of us followed suit and waited for Kilby to escort the officer to the lobby.

"Has he always been a dick?" Mike asked.

"He's not a dick," Mandy started. "I've known Officer Lance a long time. He's an old school, by the book type of guy. If you cannot see it or touch it, it's not real. But he's a good homicide detective. Believe me, he wants to catch this guy...umm... woman just as bad as we do."

I checked my watch and saw I wouldn't have time to drop off Sally or change before I had to be at Meadow's.

"I'm done for the day. See you all tomorrow."

I turned to call for Sally, who was patiently waiting for me at my desk when I heard the laughter.

"Damn, hot date?" That was from Ben.

"I've never seen him try to run out of here so fast," Mandy added.

"Go get 'em, tiger," Mike said, causing the rest of the group to roar with amusement.

"Careful Mike. Your age is showing. No one says that anymore." I didn't bother turning around when I flipped the group off over my shoulder. They could laugh all they wanted. I had a date with pretty Miss Holiday. They could all suck it.

12

A date

OF ALL DAYS...

Something had crawled so far up Beth's ass, not only had it died, but it was decaying. From the moment I'd walked into the office after my session with Mandy, she'd been on my case. Her sales numbers had dropped this week, and two clients canceled their accounts after she'd missed a meeting with them. She blamed me, even though I didn't keep her schedule. Bitch. I'd heard her in her office yelling at someone on the phone; and I hoped to God it wasn't a client. If it was, I understood why people were canceling their orders and their memberships to our cloud storage service.

Beth had never been especially nice to me, but after my attack, she'd been even bitchier. And today had been no different. You'd think I'd be used to it by now, but every time she made a comment, it was like a slap in the face. I'd heard it all, from how sorry she was I was now ugly, to what a shame it was I'd never have children. The woman was down-right mean.

I held my breath when five o'clock rolled around, and she'd stepped out of her office, prepared for the verbal vomit that would spew from her mouth. But when she'd placed her reports on my desk to file she didn't say a word. In fact, she looked like she'd been crying. Her eyes were red and puffy and her normally perfect makeup was smudged. If she were anyone else, I would've asked if she was okay. But she wasn't, and I didn't. I watched in shock as she made her way to the door, with her purse hanging from the crook of her elbow and her coat draped over her arm, and silently left. No snarky comment about how lonely it must be going home to an empty house. No boasting about how perfect her boyfriend was. No bragging about how he'd been hinting at marriage. It was crazy a man would actually *want* to marry her. Today she was silent. I should've been grateful, but instead, I kind of felt sorry for her. When I thought about it, she hadn't mentioned the boyfriend in a few months.

Trouble in paradise?

I had barely enough time to get home and change before Nick came over. I rushed through closing down my computer and grabbed my bag from under my desk and headed out. Now that I didn't have Beth or work to occupy my mind, I was getting nervous. More than nervous, my palms were sweating the whole drive home, and by the time I pulled into my parking spot, I'd considered canceling.

Why was I doing this? It was a waste of time; nothing could or would come of having dinner with Nick. He was handsome, smart, and had a good job. I was sure like most men, he'd want a family. Maybe he wanted to have some fun before he settled down and found a wife. My heart sank at the thought of being filler. That's all I could ever be, the filler, the space between when a man was playing the field and ready to settle down.

Before I got out of my car, I grabbed my phone and sent a message to Veronica Venus.

Me: Am I crazy for going on a date?

VV21: Meadow? Is this you? Have you been abducted by aliens? A date?

I couldn't help but laugh at her response. I haven't been on a date in years. Hell, I barely leave the house. I'm a twenty-six-year-old cat woman, minus the cats.

Me: Yes. With an FBI agent. He's super-hot! 

VV21: FBI?

Me: Sigh. Long story. I'll fill you in tomorrow. He'll be here soon; I have to get ready.

VV21: Have fun. Be safe. And I want details tomorrow. Wait, the FBI guy from the other day?

Me: Yes.

VV21: Sweetie. Are you sure it's a date and he just doesn't want more information from you?

Ouch! As much as what she said stung, maybe she was right. Was I making too much of this? Nick asked if I wanted to grab dinner. He didn't call it a date. He didn't even ask, really. Just I'll come by, and we'll have dinner. Shit. I'd misread the situation.

VV21: I'm not being mean. I don't want to see you get hurt. Don't let him use you.

Use me? Nick wouldn't use me, would he? I didn't know him that well, but he didn't seem like the type of man that would be dishonest or underhanded.

Me: No. You're right. He didn't call it date. He said "dinner." I called it a date. I'm sure he's being nice checking on me since I was hypnotized today and remembered some awful stuff.

How could I've been so stupid thinking that Nick wanted to go on a date with me? He felt sorry for me, that was all. He was a nice guy, and nice guys go out of their way to help broken women like me.

VV21: YOU REMEMBERED?!

Me: Not everything. I'll message you later and tell you about it. I'm sure I'll be home early from my non-date dinner. How lame am I thought he asked me on a date?! BBL. xo

I put my phone in my purse and headed to my door. How had I been so stupid?

"Hey."

The voice behind me had me nearly jumping out of my skin. I dropped my keys and spun around so quickly I banged my hip on the door handle.

"Damn!"

"Shit, Meadow. I'm sorry I scared you. I thought you heard me," Nick said, and picked up my keys holding them out for me to take.

I hadn't heard him approach, I was too busy thinking about what a dumbass I was thinking that a man as good looking as Nick would ask me out, even as filler, I wasn't good enough for him.

"What was that?" he asked.

"What?" I looked around and didn't see anything out of the ordinary.

"That look. What were you thinking about? You went from being scared to sad," he told me.

"I did? I didn't mean to." I busied myself unlocking the door. "Come in," I offered and stepped to the side to allow him entry.

My apartment was small, but it had everything I needed to be comfortable. Well, most of the time. Except when I had nightmares, then it felt too small. A bonus was it was within walking distance to Sam's and a grocery store. I bet Nick lived in a nice place, with a big yard, in an upscale neighborhood, with beautiful people who walked their dogs on Sunday morning. They probably had beautiful people block parties in the summer too.

"Are you sure you're okay? If you don't feel like going out, we can grab take-out and stay here or go to my place."

The backtracking has begun. He finally realized what it would mean going out in public with me.

"I'm okay but staying in is fine. It's probably easier any way."

"Easier?" Geeze. Did I really need to spell it out for him? "I don't understand."

Apparently, I did.

"Listen. It was really nice of you to want to check on me. I promise I'm not going to have some weird mental break and freak out. You don't have to do this."

"Have to do what, Meadow?" he growled. Was he mad? He sounded mad, and now I didn't understand. Why was he upset? "And why would staying in be easier?"

"Really? Seriously? You want me to explain?"

"Yeah, Red, seriously."

"Do you not see the huge, gigantic scar on my face?" I unnecessarily pointed to it.

"Yeah. I see it. What about it?"

"What about it? You cannot be that dense. You're a smart man. What do you think happens when I go in public? I can't hide it. People look, and stare, and sometimes point and say shit. Everyone will see you with me and wonder what the hell the hot guy is doing with the ugly chick."

Shit. I hadn't meant to say the last part.

Nick ate up the distance in three angry strides and cupped my face in his large hands, effectively rendering me speechless. No one had ever touched my scar and Nick had done it twice now. Well, the doctor had, but he didn't count.

"Meadow, not one single person better point, stare or say shit to you when we are out together, or I'll lose my shield in a quick-hot-minute when I shove my foot up their ass. Anyone who sees the two of us together and doesn't wonder what such a beautiful, brave, smart woman is doing with the likes of me is a dumbass. Straight up Red, you need to stop filling your pretty head with bullshit. Do you think I care what other people think? Fuck no I don't. I care what *you* think. And this…" He paused and ran his thumb across my scar, "means you're alive. It takes nothing away from how beautiful you are. Your beauty shines from the inside out; scar be damned."

If he hadn't been holding me up, I would've fallen to the floor.

"Why are you really here?"

I held my breath and waited for his answer.

"Because I want to get to know you better?"

"Why?" I asked.

"Why? Do I need a reason?" I nodded my head and he continued. "Because I'm attracted to you and not just physically. But that's not to say I'm not using every ounce of willpower right now not to kiss you. I've watched you for years like some weirdo in the coffee shop, hoping that you'd give some indication you'd welcome conversation. But you haven't. And while the situation that brought me to you is fucked up, I'm not stupid, and I'm taking my shot."

Wow. He'd watched me too.

"Say something Red. Have I freaked you out?"

"Is this a date?" I blurted out.

"Yeah. It is."

"I haven't been on a date since before. No one has wanted to date me." Damn. Now I was making myself sound pathetic. Not that I wasn't, but I didn't want him to know just how pitiful my life was.

"You're wrong. Men take one look at you and know they're gonna get shot down, so they don't approach. You have a wall built around you that is a mile high and just as thick. I'm not complaining. I'm pleased as hell no one has been smart enough to saddle up with a jack hammer and break through. But it has nothing to do with a scar and everything to do with you screaming stay away. Whether you mean to or not, it's there. Just to be clear, Red, I have every intention of breaking through."

"You can kiss me." What in the ever-loving hell possessed me to tell him that? I think I was having an out-of-body experience. So, I told him just that. "I must be in some alternate universe or still under hypnosis because I think I may be floating right now. Are you real?"

"Yeah, baby, I'm real. And as much as I'd love to kiss you, we're gonna take this slow. I have a feeling that once I taste your sweet mouth, I won't ever get enough."

"Wow."

He leaned down and closed the distance between our lips and gently brushed his against mine. The contact was soft and brief, and after the touch I didn't want slow. I want now and fast.

"You kissed me," I breathed.

"Red, if you think that was a kiss, I hate to say it, but you've been doing it wrong," he laughed. "Sally's still in the car. Is it cool if I bring her in?"

"Shit, Nick. Why did you leave her in your car? Go get her." I pulled back and gave his chest a shove. He didn't move, he just stood there and smiled at me. "Are you wearing one of those bulletproof vests?" I asked.

"No. Why?"

"That's all you?" His chest felt like it was lined with steel.

"All me," he confirmed.

Damn!

"I'm gonna go get Sally before I forget we're taking this slow and throw you on your couch."

He left.

I paced.

By the time he got back, I still hadn't had enough time to wrangle my newly-awakened sex drive under control.

"Hey, sweet girl." I knelt to greet Sally. "Why isn't she coming to me?"

"I haven't given her the command yet," he explained.

"Oh. Well, can you? Her tail is wagging so fast I'm afraid she'll take flight."

With a flick of Nick's wrist, Sally barreled toward me and stopped just shy of knocking me over, waiting for me to give her love.

"How 'bout we order a pizza and stay in," I suggested.

"Meadow," he warned.

"Because of Sally. Unless she can come in a restaurant with us. I don't want her to have to wait in the car. I wouldn't enjoy my meal worrying about her."

"Is that the only reason?"

"Yes. Promise."

I didn't even have to think about my answer, it came immediately, and it was the God's honest truth. For the first time in five years, I wanted to stay home not because of my scar but because I wanted Nick and Sally all to myself.

"Sounds good. Mind if I change out of my work clothes? All I have is my gym bag, so I'll be grungy."

Nick in workout clothes? Yes, please!

"Fine by me."

Nick shook his head and smiled. I wondered if he could read my thoughts? He seemed to be awfully proficient at reading people's facial expressions.

"Sally. Stay."

Sally and I stayed. Sally, for her part, sat and watched her owner walk out the door. I did almost the same thing; only I was watching his rear end.

13

The missing piece

WHEN WE CATCH the bitch that had attacked Meadow, I hoped she got the needle. Thankfully, Virginia had one of the shortest times between sentencing and being put to death. No woman should ever be worried about the things Meadow was afraid of. I hoped like hell she was exaggerating about people pointing and commenting on her scar, but I didn't think she was. Some people were insensitive assholes. I saw it when I was a kid and a friend of my uncle's came to visit. He'd been medically discharged from the Army when he lost his leg in Iraq. People wouldn't stop staring. My uncle Nolan was so pissed, but Tony stopped him from saying something to a group of women who were being particularly rude. He told Nolan he was proud of his hardware. He'd given a part of his body willingly, and no group of hags would make him feel less proud of his sacrifice.

Maybe one day Meadow would come to understand the mark left on her face was a testament to her strength. She had lived. While her and Tony's situations were vastly different, they both endured public ridicule. Tony had embraced it. Meadow was still rejecting the idea she was still beautiful. It would be a long road, but I was looking forward to convincing her otherwise.

After I'd changed into my track pants and sweatshirt, I realized my mistake. The thin athletic pants did nothing to hide my hard-on. Not that my slacks did much better, but at least the material was a tad thicker. I'd been trying the last thirty minutes to will my dick into submission, but it wasn't listening. Not when Meadow was in a pair of yoga pants sitting on the floor rolling around with Sally.

There was nothing particularly sexy about Meadow roughhousing with the dog, but she was smiling, happy, laughing. And that just might've been the sexiest thing I'd ever seen. She was bright and carefree; it was a pleasure to watch. The sight pulled at my heart. I didn't think Meadow allowed herself to be happy often. She kept herself apart, locked away. Goddamn, the thought killed me. At a time in her life where she should be going out with her friends, living life, she was holed up in her apartment – alone.

There was never a week that passed when I didn't think about my family back in Georgia. I missed them, even after all these years. I wished I lived closer, but never more than in this moment. My family would take one look at Meadow, feel her struggle, and pull her into the fold. They'd wrap her up so tight she'd know nothing but love. I wanted that for her, which was crazy because I barely knew the woman. But after the small amount of time I'd spent with her, I knew I wanted to know more. I wanted to know everything about Meadow. I wanted her secrets, her desires, all her fantasies, and most of all I wanted her pain. I wanted to be the one that carried the load and shouldered the burden so she could live easy. I wanted all of that, and I planned to work my ass off to get it – by any means necessary.

There was a knock on the door, and two things happened at once. One I was thrilled to see, the other had me red-hot pissed. All the happiness drained from Meadow's face, and she froze, shrinking back into herself. At that, Sally immediately stopped playing and sat herself in front of Meadow, ears up and on watch.

Any reservations I'd had about Sally being a protective guard dog flew out the window.

I told Sally to stay, grabbed my wallet, and went to answer the door. Thinking it was the pizza delivery, I was shocked when I opened the door, and a woman was standing there.

"Oh. I'm sorry, I was looking for Meadow Holiday. I must have the wrong address," she said.

"Beth?" Meadow said from behind me.

"Hi Meadow. I'm sorry to bother you. I didn't realize you had your boyfriend over."

There was something about the way the woman said boyfriend that pissed me off. It was patronizing and meant to hurt Meadow. What a bitch.

"Anyway," the woman went on, "I was stopping by to apologize. But I don't want to interrupt."

"Oh, he's not..." Meadow started.

"Nick Clark." I held out my hand. "The boyfriend."

"I didn't realize you'd started dating again. I mean after you got that... you know... on your face, I assumed you'd sworn off men. I guess I'm just surprised. It's been like forever ago, and you've never talked about going on a date."

There was a low, menacing growl from Sally. I looked back to see she'd once again placed herself in front of Meadow. The hair on her back was standing at attention, and her head was low, ears pinned down.

"Easy," I told Sally and gestured for her to sit. She did as she was told and sat on Meadow's feet, not moving a fraction of an inch from her.

Good girl.

Meadow had absentmindedly reached for Sally; her hand went to her head, and she was petting her. Whether she reached for the dog needing to ease some of her own discomfort or she was doing it to settle Sally I wasn't sure, but Sally was perfect for Meadow.

"I don't wanna be a dick here, but Meadow and I are in the middle of something. Is this something you can talk about later?" I asked.

"Oh sure. I wouldn't have come over if I'd known. I'm sorry I'm so shocked. But look at you and look..."

"I wouldn't finish that sentence," I warned.

"Well. I'm just being honest. That thing on her..."

"Honest to God! Are you standing here on my woman's front porch insulting her? Holy shit lady, you're fucked. Maybe you should be more concerned about your manners and less concerned about who Meadow is dating. Not only is she ten times better looking than you, but she's got a hundred times more class. And that is part of what makes her so beautiful.

So, unless you got another apology to hand out for being a rude bitch, I'd suggest you get gone."

"I'll just talk to you at the office." Beth turned to leave and bumped into the pizza boy, knocking the box in his arms making him stumble back before he regained his footing, saving the pizza. "Clumsy idiot. Watch where you're going."

What the fuck?

"She's not worth it." In my anger, I'd missed Meadow coming up beside me. She reached down and grabbed my hand, giving it a firm squeeze. Her touch did wonders to ease some of my anger, but I was still pissed.

Meadow and I would be having a conversation about what *not worth it* meant. No one had the right to speak to her the way Beth had. But first I had to get our pizza and settle Sally down. I'd never heard her growl at anyone before. Animals had good instincts. Sally not liking her only further solidified my dislike of the bitch Beth.

"Pretty dog. Is he friendly?" the pizza guy asked.

"Her," Meadow corrected. "Yes, she's normally friendly. Unless you're a rude bitch apparently."

I was happy to see Meadow's smile was back, obviously pleased that Sally had growled and protected her against Beth's insults. That kind of pissed me off as well. Not that Sally did it, but that Meadow was genuinely pleased a dog had stood up for her. Fuck. She had no one to make her feel safe and cared for. No one to cushion the blow and take her back when the world was crashing around her. I hated that for her.

I paid for the pizza and shut the door. "Who was that?"

Meadow didn't answer. Instead, she went into the kitchen and started opening cabinets, getting plates and glasses out, setting them on the counter.

"Meadow?"

"I work with her," Meadow sighed. "She's a miserable human whose sole purpose in life is to be mean to people."

"She always that rude to you?"

"That wasn't rude. That was mild compared to how she behaves in the office."

"You're shitting me?" I asked, and Meadow shook her head. "Please tell me you are shitting me."

"Afraid not. She's like that to everyone except the boss. She is sugar sweet to him and kisses his ass. She's even kinda mean to her clients. Today she was extra pissed because she lost two accounts. The boss isn't going to be happy. Business has been down the last six months. I'm kinda scared they might start laying people off."

"Fusion Telcom, right? What does the company do?"

I haven't had time to investigate the company Meadow worked for yet. With a crazy serial killer running around and being on a clock until she killed again, I had to prioritize. Besides, I'd like to get to know Meadow directly from Meadow – not a case file. I already knew too much about her from reading police reports and medical records.

"There are two divisions, infrastructure and storage. One team is dedicated to building phone systems, interoffice networks, and security systems. The other is focused on system management and storage, both onsite and cloud systems. I work for the system management side."

"Sounds interesting. What do you do?"

"I work with four system managers. I handle their reports. I'm an overpaid secretary and file clerk."

I highly doubted that was all Meadow did, but like anything else, she tried her hardest not to draw attention to herself.

"What does Beth do?"

"She's a system manager. She's a computer whiz. Which is a good thing, because most of her work can be done remotely. As you saw, she's not a people person.

Most of her clients only use our cloud storage. Very few of our clients use onsite hard drives."

Online cloud storage?

"Do your clients use the cloud to store their security camera feeds?"

"Yeah. Most do. Why?"

"Nothing. A case I'm working on. The security feeds were deleted."

"If they were stored in the cloud, it would only take a few keystrokes to delete the file. Any employee with the login could do it. Or the system manager. Hell, even I have access to our client's storage. The only thing I cannot access is the files they encrypt, but those folders are typically the accounting files and bank information. People are ridiculously loose with their information. They think because they store it with a password someone can't backdoor in. They forget someone has to manage the system and how much data they use."

"If a file was deleted from your server is it gone forever?"

"No way. Our servers back everything up, even folders a client deleted on their end."

That was it. The missing piece I needed.

14

The Filler

SOMETHING WAS WORKING behind Nick's eyes. The rest of the world had fallen away, and he was deep in thought. It was interesting to watch; he looked like he was putting a puzzle together in his mind. Every few seconds his brow scrunched, then he'd relax, and the corner of his mouth would pull down. My favorite was when he was concentrating extra hard; he'd bite the corner of his bottom lip.

I picked up my abandoned pizza and took a bite, nudging his knee. "Hungry?" I laughed.

"Yeah, sorry. What's funny?"

"You. Has anyone ever told you, you make funny faces when you're thinking?"

"I do?" he laughed. "No. No one has ever told me that. Sorry. I didn't mean to space out on you."

"It's okay. Can I ask you a question?"

"Of course."

Nick picked up his pizza and took a bite while I gathered my thoughts. I wasn't sure how to ask without sounding like a silly teenager, but not knowing was driving me crazy.

"Why did you tell Beth you were my boyfriend?" I rushed out.

"Honestly?" He put his pizza on the plate and set it on the coffee table.

"Yeah."

I wished I hadn't asked the question. Here was the part where he told me that he only said it to stick up for me. Beth was a bully and, of course, someone like Nick would want to put her in her place. But somewhere deep inside of my belly butterflies had taken flight when he said he was my boyfriend. It was stupid. I had no chance with a man like Nick, regardless if he said he wanted to kiss me and he'd said I was beautiful. I knew my place. There was no way I'd be able to keep him, and I didn't know if my heart would survive when it ended.

"I said it for two reasons. The most important one is I want to get to know you. I want to take you out on a date and show you off before I bring you home and kiss you. I want to watch movies and eat pizza at home while I listen to you tell me stories about your childhood. I want things with you, I've never wanted with another woman. If that needs to be labeled as your boyfriend? I'm good with that – more than good actually. I don't want to freak you out, we'll go slow and take our time, but Meadow Holiday, there is something about you that has made this whole other side of me come alive. I can't explain why - it just is what it is. I'm smart enough to know not to fight it and aware enough to know you're going to fight it every step of the way. I'm ready for the battle, even if that means I have to go to war with what's swirling around inside your head. I'll fight for you, for us, for you to give us a chance. That's all I need, a chance."

I was most definitely still under hypnosis. I'd asked him before if he was real, if I was awake, and he told me he was but – I had to be dreaming.

No one had ever wanted to fight for me, not even before my attack. Sure, I'd had dates, men had found me attractive, but there was no deep connection. Not that I'd ever felt. Since the day I'd woke up in the hospital, I'd felt like my life was over. I'd lost so much, and not just my looks; my sense of security, my self-confidence, and my future were gone. The attack was my fault. I'd left willingly with someone who'd tried to kill me. How could I ever trust myself again? I was no good to myself or to someone else. But now there was Nick, saying all the right things, and I desperately wanted to believe him.

"And the second reason?" I asked.

"Because no one is going to ever make you feel *less than* when I'm around. That woman wasn't saying she was surprised you had a man because she was happy for you. She was trying to put you down and get the upper hand. And that, Red, is a no-go for me. I told her this, and I'll tell you; you are a hundred times more appealing than her, and it has nothing to do with physical appearance. You can take one look at her and know she is nasty and rotten to her core. You, on the other hand, are pure sweetness. I'd take you with a burlap sack, sleep hair, and morning breath over her at her best any day of the week."

I nodded and picked up my pizza taking a bite. I didn't know what to say and figured if I shoved pizza in my mouth I wouldn't have to respond.

No such luck when Nick asked, "Are you alright with that?"

"With what?"

"All of it."

I closed my eyes and squeezed them together, not wanting to see his face. "After... you know." I was so fucking tired of saying the word attacked. "I got an infection. Even with antibiotic treatment, there was major damage to my reproductive organs. I had to have a hysterectomy. I can't have children. I'm twenty-six years old, and I'll never be a mother."

"I'm sorry to hear that, baby."

I heard his words and the pity in his voice. I didn't want him to feel sorry for me; I wanted him to wise up and stop the madness.

"Nothing can come of this between us; you know that, right? I really enjoyed spending time with you tonight. You're a great guy, and I believe you think you mean all those nice things you said to me. But let's face it, I'm not marriage material. I'm filler. That's all I can be. I thought I was okay being that for you. But I was wrong. There's no way I can get to know you and not develop feelings. I think it's best if we walk away now before my heart gets broken."

There. I'd said it. I let him off the hook, and when I opened my eyes I figured I'd see some sort of relief on his face. After all, I was being practical; he'd want a family one day, I couldn't give that to anyone.

However, I didn't see relief. I saw so much anger I recoiled and scooted as far away from him as I could in the small space the couch would allow.

"The fuck did you just say?" he growled.

"Umm... which part?"

"The filler part," he sneered.

Oh boy, he was mad.

"You know the women you date when you're done sleeping around but not ready to settle down and get married. The fillers." I heard the words coming out of my mouth, and I watched as his eyes narrowed into two small slits, but I couldn't stop. "The woman you use to cut your teeth on, see if you're ready for a real relationship."

"I've heard some fucked up shit in my life. I've seen even more. I've seen the viciousness one person can inflict on another. But never have I witnessed someone be so cruel to themselves. Beyond that, you think so little of me that not only do you think I would use you, but you think I would use other women to *cut my teeth*. That is jacked. Everything you just said is so fucked up I don't know where to begin to straighten your shit out. You. Are. Not. Filler. Not to me, not to any other man. I still don't understand what the hell that means. Your head is so twisted you've imagined some bullshit universe where that makes sense. It doesn't. It's fucked, Meadow!"

"I didn't mean to offend you. I was trying to explain that I know I don't have anything to offer a man long term. And I've made peace with it."

My clarification didn't seem to calm him down any; he was still red-hot mad.

"Offer a man? What the hell does that mean?"

"I can't have kids!" I all but yelled, and Sally popped her head up and pinned her ears to her head. Damn, now I was pissing Sally off, too.

"And?" he shrugged.

He shrugged like it was no big deal. Like me being barren didn't make me less than a woman.

"Does there need to be more?"

"Red, I'm real sorry to hear that happened. I'm not a woman. I imagine it's difficult. And I'm not saying this to be a dick, but do you think you're the first person that's been unable to have children? It sucks, I get it. But if you want to have kids, adopt. Just because you cannot physically grow them in your body does not mean that they will be any less yours. Just so you know, that's not a deal breaker for me. I wasn't raised by my biological parents. My dad died before I was born, and my mom was in jail from the time I was eleven to the day she died. My uncle and aunt raised me, and I can promise you they didn't love me any less because I was not theirs biologically. I was lucky Nolan and Reagan were there and took me in; a lot of kids don't have that. Why wouldn't I want to give that to a child that needs it? Why wouldn't you? So, yes, Meadow, there needs to be more."

"I..." There was nothing I could say that didn't make me sound selfish or like a bitch. But he was right; I could adopt. I had considered adopting a child on my own one day. I honestly didn't believe a man would ever want a woman as badly damaged as me. Not that I would tell Nick that; he was mad enough at me already.

"Come here." He tugged my hand, pulling me to him. Actually, he pulled me over him until I was practically sitting in his lap. "I didn't mean to make you cry. I'm sorry."

I hadn't realized I'd started, but now he'd drawn attention to it, I felt the tears falling. I hated crying and didn't want him to see me so weak.

"Sorry." I swiped at the tears on my cheeks. "I hate crying. I did enough of it for years."

"Nothing to be sorry about. Meadow, you have to stop thinking the worst of yourself. You are no man's second best. You are a strong, beautiful, woman."

I snuggled into his chest, soaking up as much heat

as I could. I needed it. I needed the comfort he offered if only for tonight.

"I don't feel strong. I'm sitting on your lap crying like a baby. And I haven't felt pretty or like a woman in a long time."

"We'll change that," he said with a confidence that sounded a lot like arrogance.

"I don't see how," I argued.

Nick's hand came up, and he brushed my hair from my face, exposing the scar. When I tried to burrow my face into his chest, he stopped me and forced my chin up until I was looking into his eyes. I'd never seen eyes like his. One was green; the other was half-green half-brown. It might've been the coolest thing I'd ever seen. I was going to tell him so when he stopped me in my tracks.

"Red, one day soon I'm gonna love you so hard you won't remember a time you didn't have it. I'm gonna start here." He tapped my forehead. "Then I'm gonna move to here." His hand moved to my heart, and I felt a zap when he touched my skin. "After I know I've made you a believer, I'll move here." He brushed the pad of his thumb over my bottom lip. I fought the urge to snake my tongue out and suck it into my mouth. "I'm gonna love you so thoroughly and carefully with my mouth and fingers there will be no doubt you're all woman."

Sweet Jesus! Did he say that? I was ready to tell him he'd already made me a believer so we could get to the mouth and fingers part of his program.

15

The beauty of a text message

"HEY, KRISTY. GLAD I CAUGHT YOU."

"Whatcha got Nick? Kilby needs these cell phone records asap," she said, stopping at my desk.

"Mike and I were just talking about security feeds at the bars being deleted," I explained.

"What about them?"

"Can you pull where the bars stored their feeds? I'm looking for crossovers on any cloud servers."

"Sure. It will take me about an hour. If I remember, all but two used offsite storage."

"Thanks. 'Preciate it." Kristy hurried off in the direction of Kilby's office, and I turned back to Mike. "How are your girls?"

"Doing okay. Janey is taking it the hardest. She called last night to complain about Donna's new man. She graduates high school in a month and wants to come live with me over the summer before she leaves for college. I told her I'd love that; Donna pitched a fit. Once Catherine and Victoria heard the idea they wanted to come too, which led to the conversation about living with me during the week and staying with their mom on the weekends, to which Donna went postal and told the girls over her dead body."

"Shit Mike. That'd be great, the girls living with you," I told him.

"It would. I'd love it. But the truth is." Mike stopped and looked at the ground and shook his head. "Donna might be a lot of things - a cheating bitch being one of them, but she's a good mom. I know the girls are upset about the divorce. However, I don't want them to lose their mom. They've always been tight; they're teenage girls, they're gonna need her more and more. Not that they don't need me, but their momma is important. And trying to talk to Donna about the fact that her bringing a man around so soon is upsetting her girls is like talking to a brick wall. All she says is I'm jealous, then breaks out into a tirade of how I wronged her and all the things I didn't give her, making everything my fault.

I'm at a loss man. There's no reasoning with the woman."

"You're a good dad."

"I'd cut my arms off for those girls. From the minute Janey was placed in my arms, I knew my world had changed. There was this little girl that needed me for everything. Having kids is life changing man."

I knew Mike was right. I'd watched all my uncles have kids; I'd seen first-hand how a tiny baby could bring the toughest man to his knees. I'd never thought about having kids of my own, not in any real way. Sure, I wanted them and figured one day I'd have them. But until Meadow, I'd never considered what that would be like, and biologically she couldn't have any. I'd told her about Nolan and Reagan raising me, and I wouldn't mind adoption. The words flew out without thought as soon as I saw her pain. However, as I laid in bed that night, I really considered what that would mean - not having a child of my own. The thought stung. The more I contemplated, I realized that was Meadow's reality, and awareness kicked in. My heart ached for her. The way she told me she couldn't have kids, with her eyes screwed shut like she couldn't bear to have them open when she said the words, told me she'd wanted children. Not being able to have beautiful daughters with shiny red hair and green eyes made my insides hurt. However, I knew deep down, if I could convince her to take a chance with me, and Meadow and I went the distance, there was a child out there that needed us. A child I would welcome and love.

"I guess it would be."

"I'm gonna run some of the doctors Joel and Ben found. You wanna grab some lunch in a few?"

"Another time? I'm gonna call Meadow and see if she wants to meet."

"Ah, yes, the beautiful Meadow. How'd dinner go last night?"

Suddenly, gossiping like teenagers became more important than his reports. He sat on the corner of my desk waiting for details.

"I don't know where to begin. It was eye-opening. I knew it was going to be an uphill battle getting close to her, but man, I didn't expect World War three. She had some bullshit in her head about being filler," I explained.

I was getting pissed all over again. After I left Meadow's last night with a kiss and a promise to call soon, I replayed her words over and over. Filler? What the fuck.

"What the fuck is filler?" he asked, just as confused as I was when she told me.

"She says *fillers* are the women who men find

when they've had enough sleeping around but aren't ready to get married." Mike chuckled. "What's funny."

"I've never thought about it that way, but she's not wrong."

"What the fuck! Meadow is not filler."

"No, not Meadow. I get that. All I'm saying is I understand her logic."

"I do too," Joel added, joining our conversation. Christ. Were these two insane? There was no such thing as filler. I took a breath, trying to lower my blood pressure when Joel spoke. "I'm not saying her logic isn't fucked up. No woman should ever call themselves filler, but I can track her thinking. Remember when I told you I knew Ellie was the woman I was going to marry the minute I saw her?"

"Yeah, but you waited two years to ask her out," I answered.

"Right. Do you think I was a monk for two years? I wasn't. I still dated, still slept around. I'm not bragging and not proud of what I did, but I was young. I knew myself, and I wasn't ready for a long-term commitment. In the two years I dated other women, I knew I'd never fall in love with them, I would never offer them anything more than a few months. I already knew Ellie was it for me. I simply wasn't ready for her."

I thought about what Joel said, and I could understand what he was saying, but it was still jacked.

"So, you fucked other women knowing that the woman you wanted to spend your life with was right in front of you?"

"Yep. I knew I needed to get all the childish bullshit out of my system before I could go to Ellie as a man, not a boy. I was still at frat parties every weekend. I had to finish school, and yes, I had to sleep with other women. I'm not saying I was some sleazeball, but there were a few. If I hadn't grown up and waited, I knew I'd wonder if I was losing out on the college experience, or if there was something I was missing. I know myself. I needed to be the man she needed because she deserved nothing less. Ellie is... everything. I never stopped watching and waiting."

"Quite the chance you took. Ellie is a beautiful woman. You're lucky someone else didn't scoop her up," Mike laughed.

"I was never worried. There was no way she could ever fall in love with someone else. Not when the connection we had was so strong. She needed to live and grow too. Besides, look at me, you think another man could stand a chance?"

Mike and I both laughed at Joel's arrogance. He was a good-looking man, but Ellie? She was stunning and brilliant. Joel had definitely married up. Dr. Ellie Brinkley worked for the CDC here in Virginia.

"I'm not saying you think of her as filler, and I never thought of any of the women I dated that way. But her? Her self-esteem the way it is, I can see why she feels that way," Joel added.

"I hate she feels that way. She told me about her hysterectomy. I didn't tell her I already knew. That's another thing, she feels like she has nothing to offer a man because she can't have kids."

"Adopt." Mike shrugged, mirroring my thoughts.

"That's what I told her She has options but can't see past the fucking scar on her face. As if it matters - she's still Meadow, and anyone that can't see past it is a fucking fool." Mike and Joel stood speechless staring at me with matching grins. "What?"

"I know I asked you this before, but are you sure you're ready for her? A woman like Meadow isn't looking for a quick romp," Joel asked.

"I've had my fair share of women. I've never been a one-night stand kinda guy. I like knowing who I'm taking to my bed. But that's not to say I haven't done it. Am I ready to get married? Shit, I just met her, I can't answer that. However, now that I know there is a Meadow Holiday out there in the world, I can't stop thinking about her. I want to learn everything about her. Hell, I want her to know everything about me."

"You've got your work cut out for you," Mike noted, unnecessarily I might add. I'd already known, but last night nailed the point home. I was going to have to battle it out.

"Damn Boy Wonder, go big or go home, right?" Joel laughed.

"She's worth it," I told them.

"Then fight and don't stop until you erase all the nonsense from her head. While talking about your lady love has been exciting, I got work to do. Mike, you coming?" Joel pushed away from our group and waited for Mike.

"Yeah, I'm coming," he answered, then said to me, "dig in deep. Dig in so fucking deep she can't get you out."

I watched as the guys walked away and thought about what they'd both said. Mike was right. I was going to dig in so deep she'd never want to get me out.

I grabbed my phone and pulled up the messaging app, opened a new text box, and put my plan into action.

Me: Free for lunch?

I'd decided last night I wasn't going to play games. I wanted Meadow, and there was no sense in fucking about. I didn't need to play it cool and wait a few days before I reached out and set up another date - Meadow didn't need that either. She wasn't the type of woman that you kept waiting.

Meadow: Today?

Me: Yes. Today.

Meadow: You didn't get enough of me being a blubbering mess last night? Are you a glutton for punishment or a closet masochist? FYI – I don't know how to wield a whip.

Damn, she was funny.

Me: Lucky for you – I do.

There was a pause before my phone beeped. I hadn't realized I was holding my breath until I opened the message.

Meadow: I'm not sure if the flip-flop in my belly is because I should run and hide under my bed or if the thought of you with a whip is... exciting.

Any hope I'd had to control my erection flew out the window. Fuck. I wasn't into whips and chains but the thought of pinkening Meadow's ass with my palm while I took her from behind was certainly...exciting.

Me: I don't think the guys would appreciate me walking around the office with a hard-on. Lunch? Can we continue to explore the option of leather goods over burgers? And just so you know – I'd find you if you ever tried to hide from me.

Meadow: Yes to lunch. No to talking about this in person.

Me: Why not in person?

Meadow: I can be brave over text. I can tell you things without having to look you in the face and have you see me embarrassed or shy. IDK. It's stupid.

Damn. She was adorable.

Me: Fair warning, there will be a time when this topic will have to be discussed face to face. Not real keen on the thought of you texting me while I'm daydreaming about enjoying your body, to tell me how much you like what I'm doing. I'll be there in 30 mins to pick you up.

As soon as I hit send I was a little worried my message was too crass, but when her response came back, she shocked the shit out of me.

Meadow: What's the equivalent of a hard-on for a woman? Because I'm that!

Holy shit!

Me: Wet. Red, are you wet for me?

Meadow: It is too soon or forward if I say yes?

Me: Fuck no! I'll see you in 28 mins. And just so you're prepared, I plan on kissing the hell out of you today.

Meadow: Yippy! But don't expect flirty Meadow when you get here.

I couldn't stop the bark of laughter that escaped.

"What's so funny?" Mandy asked as she passed my desk.

"Nothing," I answered. Gauging the state of my dick, I decided I should stay seated with Mandy standing there.

"Are you blushing?" she teased.

"What? No."

Was I? Shit!

"Your face is as red as your pretty woman's hair," she informed me.

Damn. A hard-on and I was blushing. What the hell was wrong with me? She'd turned me into a sixteen-year-old boy who couldn't control his body's responses.

"Did you need something? I'm leaving for lunch." I didn't mean to sound rude, but I couldn't very well stand with Mandy there, and I wanted to get to Meadow.

"Nothing that can't wait until you get back. I reviewed the session with Meadow and have some thoughts about our unsub. Find me later."

"Will do."

The last thing I wanted to discuss before seeing

Meadow for lunch was the case, though the mention of the unsub and Meadow's recorded session did wonders deflating my rigid dick.

I waited for Mandy to walk away before I made my way out of the office. Once I was safely in the privacy of my car, I allowed my mind to wander back to Meadow's text. She'd been turned on by our exchange. That was good to know; it gave me an idea how to ease her into a physical relationship. I'd never done it before, but I was a quick study. There was no doubt I'd pick up on the finer points of good old-fashioned phone sex in no time. My dick started to throb in my slacks at the mere thought of having Meadow touch herself at my command.

16

XXX

NOTHING, I mean nothing, could pull me off the cloud I'd been floating on since Nick texted me. Not even Beth. She'd made one nasty comment after another today. This morning she was in her office when I got to work, which was unusual, but it did happen. However, today she made a point of coming out and greeting me; that had never happened. Before I had the chance to stow my purse, she'd started in. Where'd I meet Nick, what did he do, did I know how good-looking he was, people would stare when they saw us together and wonder what was wrong with him. She was relentless. I was getting ready to tell her to shove it up her ass when the boss came in, and she turned to sugar. The same way she always did. They'd gone into her office, and after he'd left, she stayed holed up in her bitch lair and hadn't emerged since.

Thank God!

I had approximately two minutes until Nick said he'd be here to pick me up and my belly had decided now was the right time to start doing somersaults. I couldn't believe I'd sent him those texts. I'd never admitted to a man I was turned on, and I certainly never texted like that. It wasn't exactly sexting, but it was skirting from R to maybe one X on the XXX rating scale. I was kind of proud of myself. Not that I'd have the gumption to say anything like that to his face, but maybe I could flirt a little over text with him.

I could smell his cologne before I looked up and saw him standing in front of my desk. Beth was right about one thing – he was damn good looking. Way out of my league. He filled out a suit with his broad shoulders and trim waist. I'd felt how strong his chest was and his thighs were just as muscular. He was a fitness model rolled up in an FBI agent package.

"Red?" Nick chuckled. "You okay?"

"Caught me staring," I blurted.

"I don't mind one bit. I'm finding I love it when your pretty green eyes are on me," he said.

"Holy crap," came from behind Nick. When he turned, Rory came into view.

Now she was more in his league, and suddenly I felt out of place. She was taller than me, had a killer body I knew she worked hard to keep, and her skin was flawless and made up perfectly. In short, she was everything I wasn't. Whole.

"Sorry." Rory shook her head and put her hand out to Nick. "Hi. I'm Rory. Sorry to interrupt."

Nick took her hand and gently shook it before pulling it away and taking a step back, putting space back between them.

"Nick Clark. Nice to meet you."

"Hey, Rory, what's up?" I asked, not wanting to be rude but wanting this conversation to move along quickly.

"I was coming down to see if you wanted to go to lunch with me and some of the girls," Rory explained.

"Sorry. I have plans, but thanks."

"If those plans include Mr. Clark here, I'd turn down the offer too." She stopped to wink before she finished. "Enjoy lunch."

The way she said lunch had me rolling my eyes. She made it sound like lunch was code for a covert sex operation. Geeze. Not that I'd be entirely opposed to covert sex after Nick's text but... Nick's chuckle pulled me from my thoughts.

"Thanks, we will," he answered.

"Meadow!"

Holy shit, what now? My desk was turning into Grand Central Station. All I wanted was to escape this place and enjoy my lunch hour with hot Nick, but now Queen Bitch Beth was bellowing my name as if there was a football field between us and not twenty feet.

"Yes, Beth?"

"I need the Hoppers file when you get back from lunch," she demanded.

"No problem."

I didn't bother waiting for a reply. I pulled my bag out of the bottom drawer of my desk and yanked when the strap caught on the metal, causing the cheap leather to tear.

"Crap!" I picked up my now broken purse and secured it under my armpit, determined to get the hell out of the office.

"I told you, you need to stop buying those cheap knock-offs and invest in a high-quality purse. My Coach bag would never rip like that," Beth chastised.

"Good for you," I mumbled and made my way to Nick. "Save me. Hurry, let's run to the elevator before something else happens."

Nick's answer was to lean down and brush his soft lips against mine, stopping to linger just a moment before looking at me. "I'll always save you, Red. On three we'll make a break for it."

I appreciated his humor and the accompanying smile made the shit Beth had slung, Rory's appearance, and my broken purse melt away. Nick was here. We were going to get lunch together. And he'd promised to kiss the hell out of me.

Best day!

As soon as we got to the sidewalk, Nick grabbed my hand and held it on the short walk to the burger place. How could a gesture so small and normal feel so big? I was giddy at the contact, and it wasn't because I hadn't held a man's hand in so long, it was because it was Nick. Last night after he went home, I'd plopped back down on my couch, picked up the throw pillow he had been leaning against, and held it to my face. In a total stalker move, I inhaled, breathing in his scent, and wondered what the hell I was doing kissing Nick. Albeit, it was only a peck, not a passion-fueled duel of the tongues. But still. I wondered if I was latching on to him because he'd extended a branch of hope and he was nice to me? Was I so desperate for attention I'd imagined things that weren't there? After careful thought, I'd decided my attraction had nothing to do with my attack, the lack of affection, or anything else negative. It was simply because of him. I didn't want him to save me; I wanted him to kiss me and touch me, and do all the other things he said he was going to do because I was a twenty-six-year-old woman. There was nothing wrong with what I was feeling toward him. And I'd also made up my mind to stop over-thinking everything. He'd said my scar didn't bother him. I was going to believe him. I had to if I was ever going to escape the self-imposed prison I'd locked myself in.

Bottom line? I was tired of feeling sorry for myself. Nick had opened my eyes to another way and now that they were opened I couldn't bring myself to close them again.

"You're quiet," Nick commented as he opened the door to the burger place offering me to enter.

"Sorry. I didn't mean to be." Damn. I was so used to being by myself I'd forgotten to talk. "I suck at small talk," I admitted.

"I'm not complaining. Is everything okay? Is Beth breathing down your neck?"

"Yeah. But that's nothing new."

The hostess greeted us and walked us to a booth. I sat and Nick slid in after me, scooting close. The girl handed us our menus and told us the specials before heading back to her podium.

"The boss came down and was in her office for a long time. She hadn't come back out until we were leaving. I'm sure I'll get an earful when we get back. The file she wants is one of the clients she lost."

"Hoppers? Isn't that a restaurant?" he asked.

"Yeah. A bar and grille type place. There are three of them in the area. They have a new point of service system they put online. It makes updates to the menu, pricing, and specials. It only has to be done at one location and is pushed through to the rest. She lost the account. All three bars. I heard the boss was pissed; it was a big account."

"I guess he would be."

The waitress came and took our order. Nick being the gentlemen he was had me order first. When we were done, the server smiled and hurried away. It was after she'd left the table that it dawned on me she hadn't looked at Nick like there was something wrong with him. The hostess hadn't either. Neither of them flinched at the sight of my face or made comments. All these years I'd let Beth's words get in my head and take root, then it budded, and before I knew what was happening, a huge bush had grown. A big ugly bush of self-doubt and loathing. It wasn't Beth's fault; it was mine. I'd allowed it to happen.

"Where'd you go?" Nick squeezed my knee, and

when he released his grip, he kept it there. Finding I didn't mind his hand on my leg; in fact, I loved it, I left it there.

With the realization people were not looking at us or pointing at me, and with a new-found confidence, in a bold move I put my hand over his and smiled.

"Nowhere. Tell me about Sally and how you got involved with Homefront."

Over lunch, Nick told me how after he'd gone home to Georgia a few years ago, he'd met one of his uncle's friends, Brian, and his companion dog. His Uncle Nolan and Brian served in the Army together. Nick said after he'd listened to Brian tell his story of returning from deployment and separating from the Army and how hard it was to adjust back into civilian life, Nick knew he wanted to be involved. He explained because Brian didn't have what the military considered PTSD, he hadn't qualified for much help from the VA. A friend of Brian's hooked him up with Homefront, and they'd paired him with a dog. That was all Brian needed, a small comfort; the loyalty of a dog and the security it brought to help ease his anxiety. Nick called Homefront as soon as he got back to Virginia and started his training immediately. Within two months, he had his first shepherd.

The amount of training Nick had to go through to

become a dog handler was crazy. I was so impressed by his hard work and dedication to both the Vets and the dogs. He'd already fostered four and Sally was his fifth. He was waiting for Petty Officer Gabe Rowling to recover from his latest surgery to take Sally. The placement was supposed to happen last month, but Gabe had a complication with his last surgery. Sally also required additional training. Gabe had complete hearing loss; while he could still speak, he was self-conscious about doing so and opted to learn ASL. Sally is trained in both verbal and hand commands, as well as trained to alert her owner of sounds and lights.

She was a smart pup. I'd miss her, but knowing what Gabe was going to gain from her made me feel kind of bitchy for wishing Nick could keep her.

Before I was ready, it was time to head back to work. Nick had snatched the bill from the table and the waitress was prancing away with Nick's credit card, laughing as I tried to call her back over to take mine.

He grabbed my hand the same way he had on the walk over and threaded his fingers between mine. Every couple of feet he'd bring our joined hands up to his lips and kiss the back of mine. I was surprised how small my hand was in his. That, of course, led to me scrutinizing his height. I only came up to his shoulder, and I was in a pair of strappy wedges giving me an extra couple of inches to my normal five-feet-five inches. His bulk, coupled with his height, made me feel safe walking next to him. He chatted about his buddies from the FBI, telling me he was the youngest agent of the bunch. I'd already guessed he was by the way all the other men in his unit were beginning to gray. I'd also assumed correctly we were about the same age. I was older than him by only a couple of months.

"So, I'm a cradle robber?" I joked when we got to the elevator.

"I'd hardly call a month and a half robbing the cradle." He held his arm out for me to proceed and waited for the doors to close before he continued. "Have you ever made out with a younger man?" he asked.

He turned, caging me in with his palms on the metal behind my head. I didn't have a chance to think, let alone answer before his lips were on mine. It took a moment for the shock to wear off before I remembered to open my mouth when I felt his tongue grazing the seam of my lips.

I opened, and he deepened the kiss, taking it from sweet to three-alarm hot in two seconds flat. Holy shit. My world was spinning, and I struggled to keep up. His tongue glided and twisted with mine, and I fought to catch my breath as he took what he wanted, forcing me to follow his lead. The elevator came to a stop, and Nick pulled away, using his thumb to wipe my lip.

"Wow," I whispered, trying to regain my composure.

"Red?" he called.

I had to blink several times before his face came into focus. "Yeah?"

"The door's open. Come on."

He tugged me close to him and guided us off the elevator into the reception area. He stopped but didn't release me. "Thank you for lunch."

"I should be thanking you," I corrected.

"I have to take Sally to meet with the trainer tonight. Can I call you later?"

I thought about playing it cool and shrugging off his question like it was no big deal. But one thing I really liked about Nick was he didn't leave me guessing. He said he was going to call and he did. Well, he sent a text, but he'd done it the next day after our first date. He didn't give me time to wonder if he liked me or talk myself out of what I felt. He deserved the same in return.

"I'd like that."

"Good. Come on. I'll walk you in before you're late and Beth gives you more shit."

He bent down and gave me a soft peck before he

grabbed my hand and steered me through the double doors and didn't let go until I was safely at my desk.

With another kiss and a promise to call, he was gone.

I stowed my broken purse, reminding myself to stop by the mall on the way home to buy a new one and pulled out my cell.

Me: Date number two in the books.

The response was immediate just as I knew it would be.

VV21: What? When?

Me: Lunch today. Sigh. I think I'm in love.

VV21: WHAT?! Love? Isn't it too soon for that? Meadow, you need to be careful. You don't know anything about him. And remember he needs something from you. Are you sure he's not using you? Sounds too good to be true.

I stared at the screen in disbelief. I'd thought Veronica Venus would be happy for me. I was hurt she was so negative about my relationship with Nick and this was the second time she told me he was using me for information.

Me: Stop worrying. It was a turn of phrase; I'm not really in love with him. Back at work. Talk later.

So, that might have been a small white lie. I wasn't in love with Nick – Veronica Venus was right, it was too soon for that - but I was well on my way to falling. I could definitely love him, and the thought gave me butterflies.

"Meadow! The reports," Beth yelled from her office door.

Sigh.

Why was Beth always so miserable? Would it kill her to smile every once in a while?

"Coming," I answered, and sent one more text.

Me: Best kiss ever! To answer your question in case you were wondering – no, I've never made out with a younger man. Or anyone in an elevator before. I approve. We should do that again, and SOON. Have fun with Sally tonight. Give her a scratch for me. xoxo

I turned my phone off and tossed it in my drawer and grabbed the file Beth wanted. With a deep breath, I prepared to enter the den of doom and gloom, reminding myself it didn't matter what Beth said to me, it never had, I was happy. I wouldn't allow her to steal that from me.

Not today.

Not ever again.

I was back!

17

I'm there

THE LAST FEW WEEKS, the Butcher case notwithstanding, have been nothing short of a miracle. Watching Meadow slowly come back to herself was a thing of beauty. Each time we'd gone out, her confidence grew. On our first lunch date, I saw the shock on her face when the hostess and waitress didn't pay us any attention. I watched as she worked through her emotions, every thought played across her pretty face but I didn't tell her I saw. Now, she seemed to take it in stride that no one treated us, or her, any differently when we went out in public. I'd tried to mask my surprise when we met at Sam's this morning, and she had her hair pulled back in a ponytail. Something so small was a huge step for her. Meadow always wore her hair down over her shoulder trying to use her shiny red locks to cover the scar on her face. Today? Today she wore it up, not trying to hide. I was so proud of her. So damn proud I couldn't resist taking her in my arms in the middle of the coffee house and kissing the hell out of her.

Another thing that had changed was, our text messages had become increasingly X-rated. She was driving me crazy with her suggestive messages. She still couldn't bring herself to flirt with me in person, but I kind of liked that she was sweet and shy in person and a sexy minx over text. The contrast drove me wild. She didn't know that tonight after I dropped her off after our date I planned on speeding home and calling her. We were going to take the next step from text to phone sex. I was taking our physical relation-ship at a snail's pace. I deserved a gold medal for rebuffing her advances. Kissing had turned into full-on make-out sessions on either my couch or hers. I'd limited touching to over our clothes, even when she tried to get sneaky and push her hand under the elastic of my track pants. I'd stopped her and kissed her silly. It was killing me, but I needed to know she was ready. I had to know without a doubt she no longer believed herself to be filler. I was falling in love with her, and it would crush me if she thought I was using her.

"Christ! You're beautiful." I looked up from the pile of mail on my table in time to watch her walk in the living room.

We'd spent the day with Sally at the dog park. The entire time we were there, Meadow was happy and playing with Sally. I still hadn't told her that Gabe was ready, and Sally would be leaving the week after next. She was going to be crushed, she and Sally had grown close. Selfishly, I wished we could keep her. The dog did a world of good for Meadow.

An hour ago we'd come home to drop off Sally and get cleaned up for dinner. And holy shit did Meadow clean up well. She'd let her hair out of the confines of the band, and it fell in waves down her back, giving me an unobstructed view of her cleavage. Since I'd met her, she always dressed very conservatively, never wanting to draw attention to herself. The short black dress with a neckline that scooped down showing off her impressive breasts was not going to allow her to blend in. Men and women alike wouldn't be able to help but notice her. If the dress wasn't enough, the sky-high red heels were sure to turn heads. Fuck! I wasn't going to be able to keep my hands off her.

"Too much?" she asked.

Her rosy cheeks and flaming red hair were too irresistible. I abandoned the mess on the table and moved to her.

"No. Never too much. You are a beautiful woman. It doesn't matter what you wear, but this? Holy shit, Meadow, I'm reconsidering going out. There's no way I'll be able to control my hard-on." She smiled and lowered her eyes. "Does that bother you? Knowing I'll be sitting across from you all night rock hard because I'll be imagining what you're wearing under that dress?"

"No," she whispered.

"Look at me." I waited until she lifted her eyes to me. "I love that you're so shy. Christ, you make my dick throb when you blush and turn away at the slightest hint of me having an erection or when I know you're turned on by something I've said. But Red, I want to see your pupils dilate and your face flush. I want you to look at me when I tell you that I cannot wait to taste every inch of your body. I need you to see what you do to me. You drive me wild, Meadow. I'm looking forward to the day when I can watch you come apart in my arms. I don't want you to hide from me, not anymore."

She nodded and licked her lips before she replied. "I'm...umm...not used to feeling sexy. But you make me feel like I am. I promise it has nothing to do with...you know...even before I never thought of myself like that. I'm nervous because I want it to be good for you, but I'm scared I won't be any good at the sex stuff. I want to be. Every time we kiss on the couch I want more, but you always stop."

"I stop because I want to take this slow with you. I need you to be a hundred percent comfortable with what we're doing and where we're going. I want nothing more than to sink into you, baby, trust me. But it's more than physical. I don't just want you tonight and a few nights after. I want to go the distance. I'm in this for the long run. I won't take you until I know you're there with me."

"I'm there, Nick," she pouted.

So goddamned cute.

"Almost. We're almost there, Red. Besides, think how good it's going to be when we finally make our way to a bed. Anticipation."

"Fine. But I want it on the record; I'm ready now. Will you kiss me before I put on my lipstick?" she asked, then raised her head fully to hold my gaze. "And just so you know; all night when you're sitting across from me I won't be able to stop thinking about your hard-on, and how it will feel in my hand and in my mouth when you finally lift the sex moratorium."

Jesus H. I couldn't believe my ears. I might've shaken my head a few times to knock the surprise of her words clear before I gave her the kiss she asked for.

Each time we'd kissed was no less exciting than the last. In fact, they got better and better. Meadow was more confident, bold, and trusting. Her tongue danced with mine, and when she bit my bottom lip, I nearly lost control. My hand tightened in her hair. Tugging, I tilted her head, giving me a better angle to fully control the kiss. Damn, she tasted like heaven, and in a moment of weakness I broke the kiss so I could finally taste her neck. Dipping lower, I ran my tongue across the exposed flesh of her cleavage. She had great tits, and the thought of sucking and biting her nipples until they were hard peaks had my dick throbbing and begging for relief. With a final peck on her lips, I pulled back and had to take several calming breaths before I could talk.

"We need to leave the house, now. While I still have enough self-control."

She didn't answer. Instead, she nodded and followed me to the door.

———

THE RESTAURANT WAS PACKED, leaving us to wait at the bar until our table was ready. I was a little surprised when Meadow ordered a beer; I took her for more of the wine type. When I told her so, she laughed and explained that wine made her sleepy, and if she was sleepy she'd start thinking of crawling into her bed, which would lead to thoughts of us getting into bed and me licking her all the places I'd promised. She wasn't doing my dick any favors. It still hadn't fully softened after our kiss, and after her whispered admission, I was rock hard again.

The well-being of my dick won out, and I pulled Meadow close. Taking her hand, I placed it over my erection. Keeping her hand under mine, I used it to adjust, relieving some of the pressure. Her body locked and her hand squeezed. Fuck, that felt good.

"Soon," I whispered and brought our hands up to my mouth, kissing her fingers.

"I'm not above begging," she said, low enough none of the other patrons could hear.

"There are a lot of things I'll make you beg for. Touching me will never be one of them."

"Hi, guys!"

Meadow nearly fell over the bar stool she was half sitting half leaning against when she heard the exuberant voice over her shoulder.

A shock of greenish blue hair and a huge smile greeted me when I looked from Meadow to the voice.

"Becky, right?" I asked.

"Hey, yeah. Weird seeing you outside of Sam's," she said.

Meadow relaxed and turned to the barista. "You changed the color of your hair. It looks great."

"Oh, yeah, I was tired of the purple. Mom keeps telling me my hair is going to fall out if I keep bleaching it, but, you know. One day I'll have to get a real job and do that adulting stuff. I won't be able to have crazy hair anymore. Anyway, sorry to bother you, I just wanted to say hi."

"No bother. It was nice seeing you too," Meadow told her.

"Oh, one more thing. Not that it's a big deal or anything, but my last day at the shop will be next week. I'm training the new person starting tomorrow. Make sure you come in. I want to introduce her to my regulars and teach her how you all like your coffee before I leave."

"Oh no. You're leaving? Why? My vanilla coffee will never taste the same," Meadow teased.

"I graduated last June. Mom was happy to have me stay until I found a real job using my degree. I finally did. I start in two weeks," Becky explained.

"Well, then, I guess I'll learn to love my coffee even if it's not as good as when you make it." Meadow smiled at her.

"What kinda job?" I asked.

"I got a teaching job. I majored in early childhood development with an emphasis on delayed and learning disabilities. I'm so excited. It's a great private school; I'll be in a first-grade classroom."

"That's wonderful. What a great job." Meadow's smile faltered, but she quickly recovered, the same way she did anytime something to do with children was brought up.

"Good luck! We'll be in to see you before you leave," I told her.

Becky waved goodbye and took off to join a group of girls on the other side of the bar, right fucking next to where Beth was standing. Her eyes followed Becky with a look of pure hate. Well, it was good to know Beth was simply a bitch of epic proportions and didn't only have it out for Meadow. I bet she was a lonely spiteful woman who wondered why she couldn't get or keep a man. It was everyone else's fault she was unhappy. A woman like Beth would never look in the mirror and admit her shortcomings. It was easier to blame others.

The pager the hostess gave me when I'd checked us

in for our reservation vibrated in my pocket, alerting me that our table was ready. Just in time. The last thing I wanted was Beth's presence throwing a wet blanket over Meadow's happiness.

"Come on, Red. Let's eat. The sooner we're finished, the sooner we can get home."

Meadow shivered just as I hoped she would. Tonight, I was going to walk my woman through the best orgasm she's ever had. That was until I got my hands on her. Then I'd see to it personally that tonight's was blown out of the water.

18

I'll call you

"YOU'RE LEAVING? BUT…"

Nick had walked me straight into my apartment, kissed the ever-loving hell out of me until I'd lost my mind and was so turned on I was rubbing myself against his erection. I'd finally gotten a handful of it at the restaurant, and since then all I could think about was touching it without the fabric stopping me from skin-on-skin contact.

"I want you to do me a favor," he told me, pulling back.

"Uh-huh."

"It takes me twenty minutes to get home," he informed me of something I already knew. "I want you to take a shower, slip into bed, and wait for me to call. Can you do that for me?"

I was confused why he'd want me to take a shower, but the hopeful way he looked at me had me agreeing.

"Um. Yeah."

"Good. Twenty minutes. I'll call you as soon as I walk in."

With a too-short kiss, he was out the door, leaving me standing with my forehead against the cool wood wondering what he was planning.

I rushed through a shower, grabbed PJ's, and hopped into bed. The wait was excruciating – longest twenty minutes of my life.

When my phone finally rang, I fell out of bed reaching for it; I was so excited.

"Hello?"

"Hey, Red. Did you do as I asked?"

"Yeah."

"Good. Are you in bed?" he asked.

"Yep."

"What are you wearing?"

"Wearing?" I didn't understand the question. Did he want to know what color my panties were or if I was wearing PJs?

"Yeah, babe. Wearing. There's no right or wrong

answer. I just need to know where to start," he chuckled.

"Start?"

What the hell was he talking about?

"Meadow. Answer my question. After your shower what did you put on before you got into bed?"

"Oh, my PJs. A t-shirt and shorts," I finally answered, still unsure what my choice of clothing had to do with anything.

"Are you wearing a bra?"

I nearly swallowed my tongue at his question.

"No."

"Good. Now I want you to lie back and relax. Remember what I said to you tonight before dinner?"

"Uh-huh."

"Remember I told you I'd be sitting across from you with my dick hard, thinking about what was under your dress? And before we left, I got my first taste of your beautiful tits?"

Holy sweet baby Jesus… was he… were we…

"Yeah."

"You have no idea how hard it was to walk out the door and not waste showing you off in that pretty dress. It took every ounce of self-control I had not to march us down the hall and taste you all over. When you told me you were thinking about touching my dick and sucking me off, I nearly came in my pants. The thought of my cock in your mouth is so fucking sexy; I'm afraid to touch my dick right now. And at the bar when you said having a glass of wine would make you think about us crawling into bed together? Well, you felt how hard you made my dick."

He stopped talking, and I heard the rustle of clothes on his end. I was tingling all over, a little scared, excited, and a whole lot turned on. I'd never done this. I'd never had the courage to talk dirty before. Was I supposed to say something to him? Was I supposed to touch myself too? There was no way I would be able to stop myself if he kept talking.

"Meadow, baby, I want you to push just your shorts down your legs."

"Okay." I did as he asked. "Are you...um... naked?" I managed to squeak out.

"Yes."

Holy fuck. Nick was naked! And on the phone with me. Naked. The thought caused another wave of heat to rush through my body. I untangled my shorts from my ankles and kicked them off the bed. The chill of the room did nothing to cool my fevered skin.

"Are you comfortable?" he asked.

"No."

"No?"

"Uh-uh," I answered.

"Why not, Red. What's wrong?"

"Because I'm so turned on I ache, and you're at your house, and I'm here at mine."

"Ah. We'll take care of the ache, Red."

"But I want you here," I whined.

"If I was there what would you want me to do?"

"Touch me," I whispered.

"Touch you? Where baby? Where do you want my hands first?"

"Between my legs?"

"Uh-uh. I'll start a little higher. I can't wait to feel your skin pebble with goose bumps as I trail my hands around your breasts, feeling their weight as I squeeze and massage them. Jesus, you have great tits, baby. I cannot wait to touch them. I'm going to trace around your nipples with my tongue until they're tight buds standing at attention, begging for me to suck them. Only when I get my fill, and I have you panting with need, will I move lower to your belly, tasting your skin, kissing and nibbling my way farther down. Tell me, Meadow, are you touching yourself?"

Sometime between when he'd started talking and when he'd asked, my hand found its way between my legs. I ran my hand over the outside of my panties, unbelieving at the wetness I could feel.

"Yes."

"Where?"

"Outside of my panties," I told him, completely unashamed.

"Slide your hand inside your panties. Touch yourself." I did as he asked, pushing the scrap of material to the side and touching my fingers to my wet flesh. "What do you feel?"

"Wetness," I told him. His answering groan spurred me on. "I'm drenched and hot. I wish you were here to touch me."

"Me too, Red. Soon. I can't wait to taste you and fuck you with my fingers as I lick you from slit to clit. Push one finger inside, baby."

"Oh, God!" I did as he asked, and my inner muscles contracted. "Shit that feels good."

"I'm gonna touch myself Meadow. This is going to be quick. My dick has been hard and aching for you all night. I want you with me. Are you ready?"

"Yeah, I'm ready."

I was so ready!

"Fuck Meadow. My dick is so goddamn hard thinking about you touching yourself. Pull your finger out and rub your clit for me."

"Nick."

"That's it, Red. Rub yourself. I want to hear you."

He was silent for a moment, and I concentrated on the feeling between my legs. I could hear him breathing, and the faint sound of movement.

"What... what are you doing?"

"Trying my hardest not to come as I stroke myself, imagining how sexy you're gonna look when I lie you on my bed, spread your legs wide and eat you. My tongue. My fingers. I'm gonna lap up every bit of you. After you come..." He trailed off for a moment and groaned, causing the first spark of spasms deep inside me. "After you come, Meadow, I'm gonna settle myself between your legs and sink my dick so deep you're gonna scream for me. You ready for that baby? For me to fuck you so hard and so long you scream."

"Yes," I hissed and rubbed harder and moaned at the building sensation.

"Meadow. I'm so close. Fuck, Red, I wish you were here to see how hard you make me."

"I'm really, really, almost there. Almost." I wasn't sure if my words were making sense or if I was even speaking English. The stir I'd felt had now turned into a roar, and I was barreling toward a cliff. "Almost."

"I'm gonna come, baby," Nick warned. Holy shit that was hot. This big, strong, sexy man was touching himself while thinking about doing a whole bunch of naughty things to me and he was going to come just imagining doing them. Damn if that wasn't enough to push me off the edge, him moaning my name as he came certainly did the trick.

I was silent for a moment while the aftershocks of my orgasm faded, and embarrassment started to creep in. I couldn't believe I'd masturbated with Nick – while on the phone. Shit. What now? Was I supposed to say thank you? Ask him if it was as good for him as it was for me?

"I can hear your mind working, Red. Relax."

"How do you do that?"

"I know you. You're wondering what you're supposed to do now. The answer is nothing. Lie there a minute and relax. Clear your mind of anything that comes close to embarrassment. You are so fucking sexy, baby, you got me off in five minutes. You know how many times that's happened in my life?"

I didn't think I wanted to know the answer to that.

"No."

"Once," he told me.

Damn, that stung. Sure, I knew he was no virgin. Anyone with a pair of eyes could take one look at Nick and know he was sex on a stick. And there was no doubt he knew his way around a woman's body. But I didn't want to hear about it.

"Oh."

"When I was a teenager and first discovered the Victoria's Secret catalog my Aunt Reagan had laying around the house," he told me.

"Ew."

"Nothing gross about learning about your body, baby. And I plan on knowing yours as well as I know my own. You okay?"

His voice held so much concern; I couldn't help the warm and fuzzy feeling that had taken root in my belly.

"Yeah. I'm okay. Thank you." Nick's laughter made me smile before I quickly added. "For talking me out of being embarrassed. Not the orgasm, you jerk. Though I guess I should thank you for that, too. It was really good. Am I allowed to ask if it was good for you too? Or does that make me weird?"

"Not weird. You can ask me anything, anytime. As for mine, there is a mess on my stomach that's damn impressive, and if you made me come any harder, I might've lost consciousness."

"Thank you for dinner. I had a great time today."

"Me too. We'll do it again before Gabe comes to get Sally."

Over dinner, Nick told me Gabe was ready for Sally. It was so hard not to be sad that Sally was leaving. Gabe needed her, and she was such a great dog. I knew she'd work her magic and help the vet adjust to his new life without his hearing. Nick explained that he would start the process of getting another dog to foster in a month. He asked me to go with him to meet Alexandra and pick up the new foster pup she gave him. I loved that he was thinking about the future and including me in his plans.

"I'd like that. Will we be able to see Sally again?" I asked.

"Not for six months. She'll need time to bond with Gabe and us being around her will lead to confusion. You're gonna miss her, huh?"

"Yeah. I don't know how you can do it. Don't get me wrong, I think what you do is amazing, but I'd never be able to let her go."

"It's hard. Especially with Sally. I've had her longer than the rest because of Gabe's surgeries and the extra training she needed. But there's something else with her too, she's... I don't know how to explain it. She just feels different than the rest. It will be hard to see her go."

"I'm sorry. I'm being selfish thinking about how much I'll miss her, and I've only known her a few weeks. You've had her a long time."

"You're not selfish Red. Listen, you get some rest. I have to jump in the shower to clean up."

I couldn't stop the laugh that exploded. I don't

know what struck me as funny, but suddenly thinking about Nick lying in his bed with a mess on his hard six-pack stomach while talking about something as normal as his dog had me in stitches.

"Yeah. I guess you'd better. I'm going to sleep."

"Goodnight, Meadow. Thank you for trusting me."

"I do. I trust you completely."

"'night baby."

"'night Nick."

He clicked off, and I dropped my hand to the bed, still gripping my phone. Holy shit that just happened. My first ever phone sex. My first sexual experience with Nick. I was back to laughing when my phone vibrated in my hand.

Damn, I was falling for him and fast. I pulled the text up, excited to see what Nick had to say and frowned when I saw it was from Veronica Venus.

VV21: You alive?!

Crap. I'd forgotten I told her I'd text her when I got home from my date.

Me: Yeah. Sorry. Late night.

VV21: So? How did it go? Spill.

Me: I'm happy. Really, really, happy.

VV21: I'm glad. I hope it lasts and you're being careful.

Hope it lasts? Geeze.

Me: I'm careful. He's an FBI Agent. I think I can trust him.

VV21: If you're happy, I'm happy for you.

That was the Veronica Venus I was used to. Supportive and kind. The last few times we'd talked about Nick I was getting annoyed that her messages seemed to warn me off getting close to him. I knew she was over cautious and was trying to be protective, but her comments were borderline rude and had me thinking she was jealous I'd found a way to finally move past what had happened to me.

Me: I am happy. Thank you for always being such a good friend. I'm beat! The alarm will be going off too soon. I'm off to bed. Night.

VV21: Sleep tight.

19

A lot like love

"IT'S THE NINETEENTH MIKE." I paced in the conference room.

Still no closer to catching the Butcher. My skin was crawling with a dread I couldn't understand. Something was off; my gut was screaming at me that something had changed. Something big and I was missing it.

"There are cops swarming the city, undercovers in bars; the news has been broadcasting the murders for the last three months on almost constant replay. Citizens know to be careful. The police have been in contact with bar and restaurant owners to inform their employees to be hyper-vigilant. We're doing everything we can," he reminded me.

"Fuck. I know. I can't help thinking she'll change up her MO if she feels the heat. She'll have to change something – I just can't figure out what it is."

"Are you sure you're not overthinking it now because of Meadow?"

"Maybe you're right. All day all I've thought about is Meadow in a dirty alley, her face cut to ribbons."

"That's not going to happen. Meadow is safe. You need to keep your head straight, so we can catch her," Mike told me.

"I know."

My frustration was mounting. How the fuck had this woman evaded the police? Fourteen kills, one victim alive. I hated thinking about Meadow as victim number one, but that's what she was. The one that got away. If she tried to come back... No! Meadow was safe.

Of all nights, the nineteenth fell on a Thursday. The busiest night for a bar in the area, busier than Friday and Saturday. The weekday rush was thanks to the Thursday night special. Most bars ran two-for-one specials or had the very popular *ladies' night* where women didn't pay a cover charge.

"Did you finish the list Kristy gave you?" Mike asked.

"Yes. Nothing. The bars did use online services for

storage, but each bar used a different host. And two bars didn't use a cloud-based service. They stored their files on a hard drive in the manager's office."

"Dead end," he muttered. "Joel and Ben are still trying to get a warrant so the doctors will release their patient list. I get HIPAA and protecting privacy, but there is a serial killer out there, and her name must be on one of those lists. The red tape is damn frustrating."

"Sure as fuck is," I answered.

I pulled my phone out of my pocket, unable to stop myself any longer. I needed to know Meadow was safe.

Me: How's your day?

Meadow: Is it illegal to tie up one's co-worker and duct tape her to a chair? A gag might be involved too. Asking for a friend....

I snorted a laugh; having no doubt that if I gave Meadow the go-ahead, she'd tape Beth to a chair. According to Meadow, Beth was on a tirade at work, and Beth didn't much like that Meadow was no longer taking her shit. The more Meadow had stood up to Beth, the bitchier she became. Which was true for most bullies. Beth no longer had the upper hand, and it was driving her nuts.

Me: Tape is not a good choice. Too easy to leave behind fingerprints. Even though, you'd look super sexy in orange, it would be a shame if I had to visit you behind glass. It would really put a damper on all the things I want to do to you.

Meadow: No tape - check. Rope? And do tell SA Clark, what types of things would you like to do to me.

Me: Filthy, naughty things. Things that would make your pretty cheeks pink.

Meadow: *squirming in my seat* details?

Me: Better idea. Dinner at my house tonight and I'll show you.

Meadow: Show or tell?

Me: Show. Pack a bag. You'll be in no shape to drive when I'm done. Not that I'd let you leave.

There were several minutes of silence, and I hoped I made the right call. Since the first night we'd both gotten off over the phone, it'd happened two more times. The last call, she'd initiated the sex. It was off-the-charts hot. I was getting hard thinking about how bold Meadow had grown. She'd been vocal telling me exactly where and how she wanted me to touch her. She moaned into the phone, explaining in great detail how badly she wanted to touch me.

I thought that was a good indication she was ready to move forward, but now after five minutes with no reply, I was questioning myself.

Me: Meadow?

Another ten minutes passed and nothing. I called,

and I went straight to voicemail. Her phone was either off, or she'd done it on purpose. Fuck.

It was the nineteenth. Meadow. Fuck. My gut twisted some more, and I dialed her office number.

"Meadow Holiday," she greeted out of breath.

"You okay?"

"Yeah why?" she asked, trying to catch her breath.

"You didn't reply to my last two texts. I wanted to make sure you weren't upset with me."

She was safe. If she was pissed, so be it. I could handle that.

"Oh. Sorry. My phone died. I had to run to my car to get my charger. That's why I'm out of breath. Before I could go, queen bitch face needed a file. Right now. Immediately. Urgent. Couldn't wait." I smiled at the way Meadow had said the last few words, sarcasm dripping in her tone. I could picture her rolling her eyes as she spoke. "Anyway. Dinner at your house sounds great and… the fun stuff too."

"Great. Meet me there at six?"

"Yes. If you're not visiting me behind bars tonight. She's crazy!"

"You can handle her. See you soon, baby."

I heard Beth barking orders in the background before Meadow sighed. "Tonight. Bye."

———

"NICK!" Meadow moaned and thrashed her head on the pillow.

"Yeah, Red?" I chuckled, knowing what she was going to say; the same thing she'd been begging me to do the last twenty minutes.

"I need you."

"I'm not done yet," I repeated what I'd already told her. She was trying to move me along. Her hands were in my hair, and she was trying to push my head where she wanted. "Baby, the more you stop me, the longer it will take. I've waited forever to taste your pretty nipples and now that I have them in my mouth, I'm not done."

"You're killing me," she whined, taking one hand from my head and trying to push it between us.

"No. No. Meadow. No touching yourself. When you come this time, it is all mine."

I bit her nipple, and she shook, calling out my name again. After a few more licks I moved my way down her stomach, not wasting any time as I trailed my tongue across her flat stomach, lower until I stopped just shy of where she needed me.

"Is this where you want me?" I asked, spreading her with my fingers, exposing her soft, wet, pink flesh.

Her legs fell further apart, giving me room to lower my mouth and give her one long lick, gathering her wetness, savoring the taste of her. "Fuck, Red, you taste so damn delicious."

"Uh-huh. Please."

"Hold on to my head. I'm gonna make you come."

Both her hands went to my head, my mouth latched on to her clit, and my fingers found her wet pussy. She was so primed and ready to orgasm it took mere minutes to make her detonate. She screamed her pleasure, and my chest swelled knowing it wasn't my words but my actions that had brought her off.

Before the tightening of her muscles stopped, I pulled my fingers free and pushed up, settling myself between her legs.

"You sure you're still okay with this?" I asked and held my dick at her opening.

I'd had a physical and Meadow couldn't have children, and it had been a long time since she'd had a partner. When I'd received a clean bill of health, we agreed there was no need to use condoms.

"Yes," she said, and lifted her hips, the tip of my dick sliding in a fraction of an inch.

I had to close my eyes at the contact and count backward from ten. When I opened my eyes, Meadow was smiling at me, face still flushed from her orgasm. I settled in deeper and gave her my weight; resting my elbows by her head, I kissed her soft and slow as I gently gave her more of me.

"Relax," I whispered against her lips when she tightened around my dick.

"Is that it?" she grimaced.

"No, baby. We'll go nice and slow until you get used to me."

I pulled back and pushed forward only giving her the first few inches, slowly working her back up. When her body relaxed, and her hips started to move, I gave her more.

"Now?" she panted.

"No, Red. You'll know. Trust me."

"Just do it."

I continued my careful thrusts, not giving her more than she was ready for.

"We have all night." Well, we didn't have that long. She felt so fucking good my balls were tightening and I wasn't even fully inside of her. She was hot and slick, and without the latex barrier, I could feel every rib and groove of her pussy. I'd never experienced sex without a condom; I was thankful Meadow was my first. "You feel so damn good, baby. Fuck you're beautiful."

I lowered my face, unable to stop from kissing her. She allowed me to control the pace of both the kiss and our love making, letting me take the lead. Damn, but I liked that too. Her hands roamed my back pulling me closer to her, holding on to me like a lifeline. Once again, the swelling in my chest grew, only this time it wasn't from pride, it felt a lot like love. My heart thundered in my chest as the realization dawned; I was crazy in love with Meadow Holiday. There was no more falling, the edge came and went, and I'd toppled over. The words were on my lips, but I held them back. The first time I told her, I wanted her to know I meant them, and they weren't said in some hormonal frenzy.

"I need more," she begged.

Thank God! She said the words I needed to hear, and on the next downward thrust, I pushed deep and fully seated myself.

"Holy shit, Meadow." It was my turn to pant when her pussy throbbed and pulsated around my dick, and I swore again.

"Please." She tilted her hips and wiggled.

"Shhh." I hitched her leg further up my hip and buried my face in her neck.

Flesh on flesh, her arms squeezing me, groans mingling together, surrounded by her smell, I let myself go and loved her as hard as I'd promised her I would. When we came together, I held myself deep inside and reveled in the fact Meadow was mine.

Later that night when she was cuddled into my side, I waited for her to drift asleep before I whispered into the dark.

"I love you, Meadow."

———

THE CALL CAME a little after 3 a.m.

Another girl was found dead in an alley.

Rebecca Krouse.

I reluctantly rolled out of bed. I kissed Meadow goodbye and told her I was called out.

The short drive from my house to the bar was spent going over everything we knew, and more importantly what we didn't know. The beautiful night I'd spent with Meadow was washed away by one phone call. By the time I pulled up, there were a dozen or more squad cars. I took a moment before I got out of the car to flip my emotions off and turn on the autopilot. I was wondering if Mike was right, was I too close to the case now that Meadow and I were together? I would be a hindrance to the investigation and ineffective if I couldn't separate Meadow from the offender.

With a flash of my shield, I ducked under the crime scene tape and moved to the alley. Mike and Ben were already there, examining what was left of the poor woman.

"Sorry to wake you, man. This one is bad. She's escalating," Mike greeted.

"Escalating? How the fuck is that possible? She obliterates their faces."

"The overkill on this one is extreme. She's... man, I'm warning you it's bad." Mike stepped aside, giving me a clear view of the victim.

Holy mother fuck!

She had no face, whatever the unsub had hit her with turned it to mush. There was blood everywhere. I could barely make out the...

"Flash your light on her head," I asked Ben. He moved his flashlight shining it back to the dead girl's head. Fuck. "What did you say her name was?"

"Rebecca Krouse," Ben answered.

Becky.

The blueish hair was stained with blood and brain matter, but it was definitely dyed an unnatural hair color.

"Anyone have her ID?" I asked, looking around for a purse.

"Yeah. Lance has it." Ben motioned to the side where Detective Lance was standing, speaking with a group of uniformed officers.

"Sorry to interrupt. Can I see her ID please?"

Without breaking his conversation with the other officers, Lance passed me Rebecca's driver's license.

It was her.

Sweet Becky from the coffee shop was victim number fifteen.

Damn! Meadow was going to freak.

20

For him... I'd do anything

I TRIED to go back to sleep after Nick rolled out of bed, but I couldn't. I knew what today was. I'd thought about it all day yesterday. Nick hadn't said anything about the day, so neither had I. It was like neither of us wanted to acknowledge the date. When the middle of the night call came, I didn't need him to tell me another person had been killed.

I'd heard him come in a little while ago and he went straight to the shower. I decided to give him time alone and got up to start a pot of coffee. I had to go to work, but I still had a few hours. I didn't know what the protocol for the FBI was. If he got called out in the middle of the night, was he still expected in the office at 8 a.m. or did they get to catch some sleep first? I also figured with his job and the things he saw, he probably needed a few minutes alone to scrub the images out of his mind, if that was possible.

I was in the kitchen trying to give myself a mental pep talk when I heard him come in. He needed me to be strong; he'd had a shit night, and if he needed to talk about it, I had to pull my big girl panties on and be tough. For him, for us, I could do anything.

He didn't say anything when he walked up behind and pulled my back to his front and held me. Damn, I was happy he was home. He stood there for a long time, not saying anything. When he released me, I turned in his arms and threaded my fingers behind his neck, not wanting to lose the contact.

"You okay?" I asked.

"No. Come sit with me on the couch."

"You're scaring me. Did I..."

"No, baby. Please. Let's go sit on the couch."

I let go of his neck and let him move us to the couch. Instead of sitting next to him, he pulled me down into his lap.

"Shit, I don't know how to tell you this."

"What's wrong?"

My mind was racing a mile a minute. What could he have to tell me that was upsetting him this much.

"This morning. We found another victim," he started.

"I'm sorry, Nick. That's terrible. The same as before? It's the twentieth, so it's her again?"

"We're waiting on a few tests to come back to verify, but it looks that way. That's not all. The victim, shit, the woman, it was Becky," he told me.

"Becky?" I only knew one Becky. "No! It can't be her. Becky, from Sam's? She was leaving to be a school teacher. There's no way it's that Becky. Right?"

"I'm sorry, baby. It's her."

"No," I denied again. "We just saw her at Sam's. She was training the new girl. She was leaving. To be a teacher. Why? Why would anyone want to hurt her?"

Nick remained silent and let me cry on his chest, holding me tighter and tighter as the tears got worse. Why Becky? Why did she have to die, yet I lived? She was going to help kids; she was so excited to start her new job. Why was I saved? I was a nobody. I would never change someone's life the way Becky would've. When I thought I'd cried all I could, I lifted off his chest, and his hand came to my scarred cheek, wiping away the last of my tears. Sometimes when I was with Nick, I forgot my face was blemished with the ugly mark. But not today. Today it was burning with the reminder of my connection to the killer, a stark memento that had someone not stopped her, she would've killed me.

"I'm sorry this happened to her," I whispered. "I liked her."

"I did too. Come on, let's get you some coffee." He stood and set me on my feet, before taking my hand and guiding us back to the kitchen. "Can you go in late today?" Nick asked.

"No. The big boss is coming down. There's a meeting at nine with all the account managers," I told him. "I was planning on being in a little early to make sure I had everything ready."

"You sure you'll be alright?" he asked.

"Yeah, I'll be fine. Thanks for letting me use you like a Kleenex."

"Anytime." Nick moved an open notebook aside and set a cup of coffee in front of me.

"What's this?" I asked, pointing to the paper and taking a sip of java goodness.

"Something for work. I thought I was on to something, but it ended up being a bust."

"On to what?" I asked, reading over the familiar names. "Sorry. You probably can't tell me."

"It's fine. I trust you. You told me if a client erased something from their cloud it would still be on the company server. I was trying to see what companies the bars were buying the cloud storage from to see if I could find a connection. But, as you can see, none of the names are the same."

"Six of those companies buy space on our servers at Fusion," I told him.

"What? What do you mean?"

"These." I picked up a pen. "May I?" He nodded, and I checked off the names. "They all rent space from us.

"Explain how that works?" he asked.

"Okay, well, let's take Chesapeake Lock as an example. They have clients that purchase space for storage. Chesapeake grew quickly and didn't have the infrastructure in place to service all their clients, so they purchase space from a larger company like Fusion. I'm making up a number, but Chesapeake buys one terabyte of space for ten dollars and sells it for twenty. The smaller company still turns a profit even when they must outsource. Now, most smaller companies use the profit to reinvest purchasing larger servers themselves, so they don't have to continue to rent space. Some don't. Chesapeake didn't, neither did Bay Broadband. Both are on your list, and both are being bought out by Fusion."

"Fuck, that's what we missed."

Nick picked up the list and contemplated the

names.

"Would Fusion have access to the files?"

"What do you mean?"

Nick's frown deepened as he placed the list back on the counter and studied me.

"It kills me to ask you this. My gut is telling me to keep the woman I love far away from this investigation, but the agent in me knows better. You're already involved and it kills me." I'd lost track of everything he'd said after *woman I love*. Did Nick love me? Was that what he was saying?

"Meadow?" he called.

"Sorry. What?"

"If this is too much for you, I'll dig in when I get to work. I should do that anyway. Never mind."

"No. I'm fine. Explain what you need again," I told him.

"Where'd you go?" I bit my lip trying to play it cool like he hadn't just rocked my world. I was afraid I'd misunderstood what he had said and didn't want to make a fool of myself if I had. "Red?"

"It's just you said *the woman I love*," I blurted out.

"And that bothers you because?"

Bothers me? Shit, I wasn't making any sense. I knew I should've kept my mouth shut.

"You love me?" There, I'd said it. My lungs started

to burn the longer Nick stared at me in silence. I couldn't find my breath as I waited for him to answer.

"Yes, Red. I love you. I'm sorry I didn't tell you before now. I wanted to, but last night after we made love didn't seem like the right time. I didn't want you to think I was only saying it because you were in my bed. I love you so damn much, I can't tell you when or how it happened so fast, but I can tell you I never want to picture a future where you're not standing beside me."

I finally exhaled.

Oh. My. God.

"Are you going to say something?" He smiled.

"I love you, too. I didn't want to tell you and scare you away. I knew when you kissed me in the elevator. I told my friend Veronica Venus I thought I was in love with you. But I lied, I didn't think I was, I knew I was."

"Come here." He didn't wait for me to come to him, he rounded the counter and came to my side, pulling me in for a tight hug. "I love you Meadow Holiday."

I didn't get a chance to tell him back because his mouth was on mine and I'd lost my breath again. By the time he pulled away and kissed my forehead, my legs were jello.

"I love you, too."

"Who's your friend, Veronica Venus?" he asked.

Over coffee, I explained how I'd met Veronica Venus on a message board for survivors of violent crimes and how over the last five years she'd been my only real friend. My safe place. As I lost my *in real life friends,* she'd stood by me, cheering me on. I left out the part where she'd told me she thought Nick was using me, and basically warned me off him. I didn't think he'd appreciate that part any more than I did.

After that, we'd both gone back to his room and gotten dressed for the day together. Unfortunately, there wasn't any sexy time, but we both had to get to work. When he pulled off his sweats and t-shirt and walked into his closet to pick out a suit to wear, I did sneak a peek at his firm ass and muscular back. Damn, he was sexy! I didn't know how I'd gotten so lucky, but for once I wasn't going to look a gift horse in the mouth. I was going to grab on with both hands and say fuck the world.

At the door, Nick handed me a to-go cup full of steaming hot vanilla flavored coffee. I loved that he had my brand of coffee in his cabinet and my flavored creamer in his fridge. It was funny how something so small made my belly flutter. It'd been doing that a lot lately, and for the first time in years, the butterflies were from anticipation of the future and not dread of the past.

"Why was Sally pacing around whining?" I asked when we got outside.

"I don't know, antsy I guess. Sally, come."

Sally finished her business on the grass and bounced over to us and sat at my feet.

"Be a good girl today." I rubbed the soft fur behind her ears. "I'll see you tonight." Crap. That was rather presumptuous of me. We didn't have any plans. "Or... umm... later... tomorrow."

Nick didn't skip a beat and tugged my hand for me to follow him to my car. He took my keys, beeped the lock, and opened the door. "You'll be seeing both of us tonight. Your place or mine?" he asked.

"Yours. I like your kitchen better, and Sally has a backyard when she needs to go out," I told him.

He reached into his pocket and pulled out a key, offering it to me. "I was hoping you'd say that. I may have to work a little late tonight. I'll let you know as the day goes on. But if I do, you'll need this."

"A key?"

I was so stupid stating the obvious. I was expecting him to reply with *no shit Sherlock*, or maybe a *good catch Captain Obvious*.

"Are you okay with that? Having a key to my house?"

"Yeah, of course. I'll make sure I give it back when you get home."

"No, Red. It's yours. I want you to keep it," he told me.

"Holy shit!"

"Too soon?" he chuckled.

"No. I may need to pinch myself again. I'm afraid this last month has been a great freaking dream. No. Wait. Don't pinch me. I don't want to wake up if it is. I want to stay asleep forever in a place where a beautiful, strong, sweet, and sexy man picked *me*. If this is a dream and I wake up alone in my bed, scared and broken with no hope of a future, I'd never survive. Not knowing what I know now. You better be real, Special Agent Nick Clark, because if you're not, my life is one big nightmare."

Nick moved, and Sally jumped out of the way when he pulled me into his arms and whispered, "You will never wake up alone again. Whether I'm lying there next to you or not, you are never alone. We are real, Red, and the future is in front of us to make of it what we want. What exactly that looks like I don't know, but what I do know as fact is - you are mine." His voice was low and husky reminding me of what he sounded like when he was moving inside of me.

"I wish we could go back in the house and spend

the day in bed," I told him.

"Trust me, I do too." He pushed his erection into my belly, and I contemplated quitting my job. A day rolling around in bed with him would be worth it. "But you have a meeting, and I have a deranged psychopath to catch."

"Damn," I whispered.

"See you tonight, Red. Have a good day at work."

He gave me a brief kiss, put me in my car, and waited for me to drive away before he got in his. I loved that too, Nick taking care of me, even if it was to watch me safely drive away.

When I pulled into the parking lot at work, I was ready to turn around and crawl back into bed. Beth was getting out of her car, and the way she slammed her door told me she was going to be on the warpath today. Geez, I hated that woman.

My phone beeped in my purse, a brand-new Michael Kors number I'd splurged on; it might not have been a Coach, but it was a step up from the cheap off brands I normally bought. I pulled my phone out and saw I had two missed texts from Veronica Venus and one from Nick.

Nick: I love you, Red. Have a good day and remember do not take shit from Beth. Tell her to shove it where the sun don't shine.

I snorted a laugh as if I'd actually tell her that. She'd probably tattle, and I'd get fired. It was amazing how my boss couldn't see through her shit. If she kissed his ass any more, she'd be milking his prostate. Hell, maybe that's what she was doing.

Me: I love you. Thanks for last night. xoxoxo

I held my breath when I scrolled to VV21. I used to look forward to Veronica Venus' messages, but these days I never knew what I would find.

VV21: I hope your sleep over went well. 😊

VV21: Please let me know you're safe. Haven't heard from you. Hope Mr. FBI man doesn't have you tied up in his basement. By the way, how is the search going? Any new leads on who attacked you? You're not going to let them try and hypnotize you again, right? I mean, it's been so long, no use in trying to remember now.

I read and reread the message a few times trying to figure out if she was trying to be protective or backhanded by bringing up my attacker. Did she not want me to remember? I decided I didn't have time to decipher what she meant, besides I had to deal with a bitchy Beth this morning.

Me: All is well. The sleepover was AMAZING. I'll fill you in later - meeting in ten minutes. Thanks for checking in.

21

I love you, Meadow

"NOW THAT'S a look of a satisfied man," Mike laughed, coming to sit next to my desk, petting Sally when he did.

"Really?" I looked up from the list of storage providers that Meadow had checked off.

"You're too easy. What's wrong with Sally?" he asked.

"Man, she's been on edge since I left the house last night. When I got home, she was sleeping in front of the bedroom door. After Meadow got up, Sally was pacing the kitchen, following everywhere she went. Meadow didn't notice until we got outside, and Sally was still sticking close. I think she's bonded with

Meadow which is going to make the exchange with Gabe difficult."

"Let me understand. You got a call out at 3 a.m. and left Meadow in your bed." Nosy bastard. I'd played right into his hand. "When Meadow climbed out of your bed this morning Sally was acting weird."

"Yep."

"How many women have you had spend the night since you got Sally?" Mike's smile couldn't be any more smug.

"None."

I hadn't had a woman in my bed ever. Not that I was a monk, but I was careful who I allowed to know where I lived. Occupational hazard.

"You think Sally's jealous?" he asked.

"I'd say yes, but she wasn't sticking to me, she was on Meadow. Hell, she whined when Meadow drove away."

"Well, you're fucked. Your dog likes your woman more than you." He laughed.

"That's a problem. Sally's not mine. She goes to Gabe next week."

"Maybe she has to take a shit," Ben added, stopping at my desk to give Sally a rub down. "I had a Golden Retriever that would circle and act weird when he was constipated."

"Really? We're talking about the bowel movements of canines?" Mike laughed. "I'm so happy I've never had a dog. That's worse than new parents talking about the color of their baby's shit."

"Since you're all here and I would like to stop talking about dog shit and my sex life, I think I found something." I pointed to the list in front of me.

"Hold up. We were talking about your sex life? What'd I miss?" Ben asked.

"Meadow spent the night last night. Though Nick's grumpy today, so either he was denied, or it was so good he's pissed he had to get out of bed," Mike helpfully told Ben.

"Shit. I'm pissed I gotta roll outta bed every morning and leave my hot wife to come in here and see you assholes. So, I can't say I blame him for being less than pleased. By my calculations, it's been at least a year since he's been laid."

I would've been pissed that Ben and Mike were discussing my sexual activity or lack thereof if I didn't find it so interesting that Ben was mostly right about the last time I'd been with a woman.

"It is a tad disturbing that you've paid that much attention to my personal life and when I'm having sex," I told him.

"The neuroscience behind human sexuality is

fascinating. You can learn a lot about a person by their sex drive, lack of, or when they're unable to find a sex partner."

"Sometimes your brain scares me," Mike laughed. "Your poor wife. Do you study her as closely as all of us?"

"Lucky for her I study her more. Trust me; she loves that I know how to crawl into her mind and pull out what I need. Besides, Nick's easy, he can't hide the symptoms of sex deprivation."

Christ.

"We're moving along," I told them. "The case." I pointed to the list again.

"The case is interesting and all. But I have to know, what are the symptoms?" Mike asked.

"My dry spell is none of your fucking business," I snapped.

Mike and Ben threw their heads back and laughed. Assholes. When Ben recovered, he said, "First symptom, extreme hostility, and bitchiness. Friend, a year is not a spell, it's a drought."

"Fuck you."

"Wow. Nice greeting." Kristy smiled and held out a folder. "I cross-referenced those names. You were right. All the bars that used cloud-based storage - while the companies were all different, when cross checked, all of the smaller companies did indeed purchase space from Fusion Telecom."

"Fuck!"

"There's your connection." Kristy smiled, and I took the folder from her.

"Conference room?" Mike asked.

I grabbed the papers off my desk and followed Mike and Ben into the other room. Sally padded along behind me, hackles still up. If I'd had time, I would've taken her home. I didn't like the way her ears were at attention and she was on alert.

"What's the connection?" Ben asked, breaking my concern of Sally.

I looked at the whiteboard. Becky's picture had already been added to the other fourteen women we couldn't save.

"Fifteen dead women. All found after a night out at a bar. Eleven on the seventh. Four on the twentieth. All security footage erased. Fourteen, if you count Meadow's attack, were stored on a cloud server; two stored on an onsite computer. Each bar used a different small company to buy their space. All fourteen of those companies bought space of Fusion Telecom servers to resell to their clients. How much you want to bet that Fusion had access to the two onsite computers as well."

I spread out the papers that Kristy had given me, Ben and Mike scrutinizing the data.

I grabbed the landline on the table and dialed Kristy's office extension, hoping she was back in her office while ignoring the knot that was growing in my gut. All the murders tied back to Fusion Telecom, the very place Meadow was at right now.

"Keep a lid on it, Clark," Mike said as if he'd read my mind.

"Hello?" Kristy answered.

"How many women does Fusion Telecom employ?" I asked, placing the call on speaker.

"Hold on." There was the sound of the tapping of her keyboard before she said, "Damn. More than I thought. Fusion has 482 employees including executives and 290 are women."

"Narrow that to single women, between thirty and forty," Ben told her.

"Okay. Two hundred and eleven."

"Still too many," Mike said. "Narrow that to women with no children."

"That will take me a few minutes," she said.

"Hit us back when you have a list," Ben said and disconnected the call. "Let me grab Joel and Mandy."

Sally roamed around the room, and the knot grew.

Fuck. I couldn't stand it any longer. I pulled my cell out of my pocket and sent a text to Meadow.

Me: Good day?

A normal everyday text. Nothing that would alert her to the fact I was ninety percent sure she worked with the woman that had attacked her and killed fifteen women.

Meadow: Better now that I've heard from you. Killer meeting. Boss is pissed. I'm going down to the sub shop to grab lunch before I'm stuck printing more reports and don't get to eat. Seems I worked up an appetite. 😉 How's your day? Catch any crazy bad guys? xoxo

Me: Glad you're hungry. Plan on packing snacks tomorrow. My day is fine. See you tonight.

Then I couldn't stop myself.

Me: I love you, Meadow. Please be careful. Watch where you're going and who's around you.

Meadow: Everything okay?

Me: Everything is fine. I just need to know you're safe.

Meadow: I'm safe. xoxo

I hoped to God that was the truth. I don't know what I'd do if something happened to her.

22

Peace offering

"IS IT TRUE?"

Shit! Rory. She scared the hell out of me again, and we almost had a repeat performance of the great mustard molestation. I had been enjoying my lunch, sitting on the bench outside of the sub shop, happy to be out of the office when Rory plopped down next to me.

After Nick had texted me, Beth stormed out of her office red-hot mad. No, she was more than that, whatever is more than red-hot mad is what she had been. The stack of files she had in her arms were tossed on my desk, and some had scattered to the floor. I was about to finally tell her where she could stick her bitch ass attitude when Mr. Klein stepped out of her office in time to witness her temper tantrum.

He pulled her back into her office, and the entire floor heard Beth screeching through the closed door. When she reemerged, she had her black designer bag hitched over her shoulder and a tight pinch on her face. She'd stormed out of the office, and Mr. Klein informed us that Beth was no longer employed by Fusion Tele-com. I guess I'd been wrong; upper management had seen what a bitch she really was. It probably didn't help she'd lost several clients over the last few months.

"Yeah. Mr. Klein fired her. He said she'd be in later to get her personal items, but he'd sent her away to cool off."

"It's about time. That woman is terrible. So, tell me about Mr. Hunk that picked you up for lunch. That's still going on, right?" Rory giggled.

Yes, she giggled like a high schooler.

"Yeah, it's still going. Nothing much to tell," I lied.

"There has to be something. Your cheeks are red. What does he do?" she asked.

"He works for the FBI," I told her, ignoring her comment about me blushing. God, I hoped I wasn't, and she was only kidding.

"FBI? Is he working on the serial killer case? Do they have any leads?" she asked.

"I don't know. He doesn't talk about work, and I don't watch the news," I told her. I would never break Nick's confidence, nor would I tell anyone that I'd met Nick because the FBI thought I was the killer's first victim. The thought made me shudder. She was still out there, killing people. She'd killed poor Becky last night.

It felt wrong having Rory ask about the case like she was. She had a look of amazement rather than outrage.

"You don't watch the news? Shit girl. There is a crazy person stalking bars. I heard that he rips off the victim's faces, can you imagine?" My hand instinctively moved to my scar before I could pull it back; Rory noticed and flinched. Damn. Not her too. "Sorry. That didn't come out the way I meant it to."

"It's alright."

The funny thing was, it was alright. A month ago, if someone had said something like that to me, it would've thrown me. I would've had to text Veronica Venus, and she'd talk me off the ledge as I cried my eyes out. Now, I found myself forgetting I had a mark on my face. I still hadn't gone an entire day without remembering, but it was kind of hard to when there were mirrors around. But I wasn't obsessing and worrying about what people thought or how disgusted they'd be at my appearance. Nick thought I was beautiful and because he did, he'd reminded me that my beauty doesn't come from the way I look. I was beautiful because I was a good person, and that was what mattered.

"So anyway. He like stabs them and leaves them for the police to find. I also heard..." She stopped and looked around before lowering her voice. "He drugs the women before he takes them. Makes it easier. No one notices because the women don't struggle. They just walk out the door with him."

How did she know that? Mandy told me that detail had been withheld.

"Are you okay?" Rory asked.

Shit. No. I wasn't okay. It was hard to breathe, and I felt weird like someone was watching me. Which I guess was stupid because there was someone watching me, Rory. She was staring at me as if I'd grown a second head.

Breathe Meadow.

Breathe.

"Yeah. I'm fine. I just feel so bad for all those girls. It gives me the creeps," I told her.

My phone beeped in my pocket, and I prayed it was Nick. I didn't want to be one of those needy girlfriends, but damn I really needed him right now.

VV21: How's lunch?

How'd she know I was at lunch? Did I tell her? I scrolled up to the last message exchange, nothing. I hadn't talked to her since this morning in the parking lot.

Me: How'd you know I was at lunch? ☺

I hoped the smiley face took some of the paranoia out of my message. I knew I was being rude to Rory, and normally I wouldn't answer a message while I was otherwise engaged, but I was feeling freaked out and completely out of sorts.

VV21: Ummm. It's lunchtime, weirdo. Besides you're a creature of habit. I could set my time by you. Desk or sub shop?

Jesus. I was losing my mind. I smiled and tapped out a reply.

Me: Damn, you're good. Sub today. I have juicy gossip!!! Have to wait until after work to spill, but Queen Bitchypants will be a non-issue from here on out. Work just became bearable. I'm done at four today; text you then.

That reminded me, I should text Nick and tell him Mr. Klein had announced he was letting us all leave early today, probably because Beth was supposed to come back after her time out to pick up the personal items from her office.

"Boyfriend?" Rory asked.

"No. Sorry that was rude." I dropped my phone in my bag. I'd text Nick later; it wasn't like it was important what time I got done, he would be stuck at work anyway.

"It's cool. So, Beth? Did she really have a freak-out?"

Geez, this girl liked to gossip. I spent the last ten minutes of my lunch telling Rory all about Beth's break down. It was petty, childish, and impolite of me to talk about Beth behind her back, but she'd been mean to me the last five years. She deserved it.

By the time I made it back into the office, everyone was talking about Beth's welcomed departure. I was so busy trying to reorganize the files that Beth had thrown on my desk I didn't get to leave at four when everyone else did. I was almost done when Beth walked in. For the first time since I'd met her, she had a look of regret on her face. The pinchy sour-puss look had been wiped clean off and was replaced with something that looked like remorse. I stood frozen, afraid if I moved the bitch would be back.

"Meadow," she started. "I owe you an apology."

"Umm." I didn't know what to say.

"I know I can be intense and a bitch. I blurt out things I shouldn't say, and I've been told more than once I don't have good social skills. Before I leave, I just wanted you to know I'm sorry for being so mean to you. You're a nice person and didn't deserve it." She stopped and placed a cup on my desk. "Here. A peace offering. A vanilla flavored coffee, extra cream, and two sugars."

Say what? Since when did Queen Bitch know what kind of coffee I liked? I eyed the cup and looked back at her.

"Thanks."

"It's the least I can do."

She smiled and walked into her office, or her old office, and started to clear off her desk. I looked at the coffee again and considered tossing it in the trash, but *hello*, it was a large vanilla, with extra cream and two sugars. I took a tentative sip making sure it was coffee and not something gross. As apologetic as she was, she was still Beth. I wouldn't put it past her to put vinegar in my drink to get a good laugh at me. However, it was delicious and exactly what I needed to finish putting these files back together so I could leave. If I left within the next five minutes, I'd have time to stop at the store and still be home before Nick.

I grabbed my phone off my desk and sent a quick text to Veronica Venus.

Me: You'll never guess what just happened?

I tossed my phone on my desk and by the time I finished arranging the last file my head was throbbing. Thank God, I was done. The excitement of the day had worn off, and fatigue had set in. I wasn't surprised, I had been up since about 3 a.m., and was nonstop busy all day. I grabbed my purse out of my bottom drawer and flung it over my shoulder. Forget the grocery store; I was too tired to cook; I'd call in a pizza when I got to Nick's.

I grabbed my phone off my desk and noticed I had a text notification from Veronica Venus.

VV21: What?

I was so exhausted the words swam on my screen as I tapped out my message.

Me: Funny story. I'm leaving work now.

I glanced at my now empty cup and was reminded I had to say something to Beth before I left. But what? See ya around? Apology accepted? Thanks for the coffee? I knew what I wanted to say; good riddance, but that was too mean. Even after all the years of torture.

Why couldn't I just be a bitch and leave without saying something?

I peeked into Beth's office, and she was on her phone, thumbs flying across her screen. She looked busy; maybe I could slip out without saying goodbye, I wouldn't want to disturb her. The moment I'd talked myself into leaving Beth looked up. Damn, eye contact, now I had to say something.

My phone vibrated in my hand, and I was given a reprieve.

VV21: Tell me, the suspense is killing me.

Me: Give me five minutes. Text you from the car.

I hit send and chanced looking back up. Beth's phone beeped, and she smirked before she looked back down. I knew that smile; it normally came right before she spewed out a nasty comment. I watched as she fiddled with her phone, my headache getting worse by the second.

I was leaving. She was busy, and I had the shakes so bad I didn't know if it was my phone vibrating or if all the caffeine I'd had was taking its toll. I needed to get home and take a nap and get rid of this headache.

VV21: Okay.

I blinked, trying to focus on the message. The small letters on the screen danced, and I couldn't focus on them.

Damn my head hurt. The more I blinked to clear my vision, the longer it took for me to pull my lids open again. I pitched forward and stumbled trying to find purchase before I hit the floor.

"Humph." I knocked into something.

"Careful, you clumsy idiot."

No.

No.

No.

I knew that voice.

23

Too wrapped up

"THERE'S nothing wrong with her. She's attuned to your emotions. You're wound tighter than a banjo," Joel said.

"He's right you know," Mandy added. "Ninety percent of human communication is nonverbal. Sally is astute; she senses a change in your body language. Research shows that canines can detect cardiac episodes and are able to alert their owners before it happens. It was originally thought it was because they could detect a change in electromagnetic waves; however, that's not the case. It boils down to smell. Humans give off an odor as a result of chemicals being released into our bloodstream before an episode or when we're anxious. You need to dial it back. She can smell you."

"How the hell can I dial it back when the unsub more than likely works with Meadow. She is in a building with a woman that not only tried to kill her but has successfully butchered fifteen other women."

"You will because that's what Meadow needs," Mike told me.

Fuck, he was right. Meadow needed me to be clear minded. I had to focus, but I couldn't. All I could think about was Meadow on the ground in a filthy alley, bleeding.

"Here are the names." Kristy trotted into the room holding up a stack of papers. She'd been working double time over the last few hours trying to narrow down names. Once the list was manageable, we'd hand it over to Lance and let his department take the lead. However, with our resources and Kristy, we'd be faster at tightening a suspect pool. "Also, I was thinking. You had me searching for newsworthy events on the seventh and twentieth. If the bodies are found in the early morning hours on those days wouldn't she be hunting the day before? The trauma would've been on the sixth and the nineteenth, right? I'm cross-referencing these names with police reports and hospital visits. I'll have the results in about a half hour."

"Fucking hell. Kristy's right." Joel slammed his palms flat on the table. "We missed it."

Kristy handed me the list; there was still at least fifty names of single women with no children between the ages of thirty and forty. I quickly scanned the list, and my eyes landed on a name.

Clumsy idiot.

Shit! I fumbled my cell out of my pocket trying to hurry and connect a call to Meadow. I had to warn her. She had to leave her office, now. The call connected and went to voicemail on the first ring - her phone was off. My stomach churned, and fear threatened to choke me. Mother fucker! How'd I miss it?

"I know who it is. Sally come!"

I didn't wait to see if anyone was following me. I had to get to Meadow. It was almost five; she'd be leaving the office any minute.

By the time I'd opened the back door of the government-issued Suburban and allowed Sally to jump in, Mike had rounded the hood and was getting into the driver's seat, and Joel slid in next to Sally, both men ready to have my back without explanation.

"Talk to us," Joel demanded as Mike pulled out of the parking lot.

"Beth Stevens, thirty-five, she is a systems manager. Remember Meadow's session with Mandy?

Meadow said she'd felt uncomfortable when the woman she was talking to called the bartender a clumsy idiot when he'd spilled a drink? My first date with Meadow, Beth showed up at Meadow's. She said she was there to apologize, that's not important, but when she turned to leave the pizza guy was behind her. She bumped him and called him a clumsy idiot."

"That's a stretch. A lot of people say that," Joel noted.

"Right. Then I was thinking about the next day; I went to pick Meadow up for lunch. She snagged her purse on her desk and the strap broke. Beth chastised her about buying cheap purses. Suggested she get a high-quality Coach bag, like she had," I added.

"I'm tracking, I remember the women talking about purses, but I have to say, you're still reaching a little. The two of those put together make her a strong suspect, but..." Mike trailed off.

"Beth is also a systems manager at Fusion; she'd have access to the company's cloud database. Meadow told me she was a computer genius. She'd have the access and the knowledge to erase the security footage. I know it's her." Sally barked, reminding me of one more thing. "How many times have you heard Sally growl?"

"What does that have to do with anything?" Mike asked.

"Just answer."

"I guess once. When you first brought her into the office, and we were interviewing the father of a missing boy," he answered.

"We thought it was because Sally was a puppy and not used to strangers," I reminded them.

"But the father ended up being the offender and buried his son in the family's backyard," Joel finished. "Strong investigative work, Nick. I'm supposed to call Lance and have his swat team surround Fusion based on your gut and a dog."

"Fuck, no. We'll go in soft. Get Meadow out and ask Beth if she wouldn't mind answering some questions. Mike, you take the lead, she's a superficial bitch. You smile at her and give her attention; she'll eat that shit up. Trust me."

I dialed Meadow's work number and still no answer. Not her cell, landline, or text messages. What the fuck.

We pulled into the parking lot, and every instinct I had was screaming something wasn't right. After telling Sally to stay, Joel, Mike, and I exited the SUV and took off toward the building in a fast clip. I needed to see Meadow.

"Hey. Nick, right?" Meadow's friend stopped us. "Rory. I met you a few weeks ago."

"Yes. Hi Rory. Sorry to be rude but I'm in a hurry," I told her.

"Well if you're looking for Meadow her department left early today. She didn't tell you?"

"No." I looked around and spotted her car still parked in the front row. "Why would they get off early."

"Funny story, Beth was fired today. She had such a meltdown; management asked her to leave and told her to come back after four to get her things. The entire department was allowed to leave early. I guess Mr. Klein didn't want anyone around to witness another tantrum."

"I gotta go. Joel, will you stay with Rory and get the details?"

I opened the double doors to the building and opted for the stairs, taking two at a time until we reached Meadow's floor. I felt marginally better knowing that Beth had been asked to leave the building. However, that still didn't explain where Meadow was. When Mike and I entered the reception area, it was empty. I headed to Meadow's desk; her phone and purse were both on her desk.

Where the fuck was Meadow?

Without remorse, I picked up Meadow's phone and started scrolling through her phone log. Missed calls from me, a call labeled mom, and more from me. Christ. Now was not the time for me to be thinking about Meadow's lack of social circle but my heart broke. She'd isolated herself so deeply the only people she's spoken to in the last week were her mother and me.

Her text messages were the same; me and her mother. No social media apps, but there was a secondary messaging app. I pulled it up and scrolled through a few messages from VV21. I assumed that was the Veronica Venus Meadow had told me about from her survivor's group. Their last exchange was at 4:21; Meadow said she was headed to her car.

I pulled out my phone and called Kristy.

"I need you to work your magic," I said without preamble. "I need everything you can find on Beth Stevens."

"Anything else?" she asked.

I told her about the message board that Meadow belonged to and the handle Veronica Venus. The mystery woman was Meadow's closest friend; I'd like to speak to her and see if she had any helpful information. While Kristy was tracking down the information I needed, I joined Mike in Beth's office, picking up a paper coffee cup and tossing it in the trash on my way.

"Find anything?" I asked.

"No. No personal items, desk drawers are neat and organized. The computer is password protected so we'll need a tech to come in to unlock it," he answered and dumped the trash can over, spilling papers on the ground. He bent down spreading them out with a pencil. "Nothing here that I can tell, normal office trash, a receipt for a vanilla latte dated today, 4:03. Nothing that screams out at me as homicidal maniac."

"A vanilla latte?" I asked.

"Yeah." Mike used the pencil to point at the receipt. "Cash receipt."

"Vanilla lattes are Meadow's favorite. I threw a to-go cup away on my way in here. It was on the floor next to Meadow's desk."

"Fuck. She drugged her. We need to call Kilby and Lance." Mike pulled his phone out to make the call. How could I have let this happen?

Within the hour Fusion Telecom was swarming with police. Adam Klein had been more than forthright when talking about Beth. Her attitude had worsened over the last four months, leading to her being fired. The time frame coincided with when the murders had started again. He'd also confirmed what we'd profiled.

While he couldn't give the exact dates, the rough estimation matched.

Five years ago, Beth's husband divorced her. A year after her divorce she began a serious relationship with a man, Brian Astro. They'd been engaged until he ended it a few months ago. Both break-ups fit. While I was pleased that more pieces of the puzzle were clicking into place, we still didn't have any idea of where Beth would take Meadow. A squad car had been sent to Beth's to sit on her house, and one had been sent to Brian's to pick him up for questioning.

I checked my watch and the noose around my neck tightened. Meadow had been with Beth for at least two hours. Two fucking hours in the hand of a depraved killer, they could be anywhere. Beth could've already butchered Meadow. I'd been so wrapped up in her I'd dropped the ball. Meadow's death was on me.

Technical analysts from both the local PD and the FBI were combing over Fusion's servers trying to recover the security footage that had been deleted. The cup had been rushed to the lab to be checked for the presence of ketamine. Unfortunately, there was no field test that would detect the drug, and we were in a holding pattern. No leads, no indication where they'd gone, nothing. I was useless standing in front of Meadow's desk, completely impotent.

Mike rushed over and Sally, who'd been brought up from the car, sat next to me. Much like she'd done to Meadow when she sensed she needed protecting. Fuck, this was all my fault. Why hadn't I seen it? My dog had a better instinct than me. She knew. Sally had met the woman one time and growled as she stood between Meadow and the threat. Which was more than I did. I'd missed every single fucking sign pointing at Beth.

"Kristy called. Lab tests came back, positive for ketamine. So far, they recovered security footage from six bars including Meadow's attack. I know you don't need me to say this, but you were right, it's Beth. Brian is talking, and they broke up four months ago on the nineteenth. He was having an affair, and she found out about it."

"Let me guess, a pretty young thing?"

"That's what he said. His secretary, twenty-two. And the husband? He cheated too. Got his mistress knocked up, after years trying to have a baby with Beth with no luck. A police report was filed on the sixth. A domestic disturbance. She'd come unglued when he was trying to pack his stuff and leave."

"Fuck!" I yelled, and Sally barked.

"One more thing. And you're not gonna like this."

24

"OH GOOD, you're finally awake. I thought you were gonna sleep through the good part."

Awake?

The good part?

Damn my head hurt. My head was groggy, and it was hard to focus. I was lying on my side in the back of a car. It was dark outside, but there was a bright light shining that had me squinting against the harsh cast. I could vaguely make out Beth's silhouette in the front seat. Why was I in a car with Beth? I struggled to sit up and nearly rolled off the backseat. Both hands shot out, and I caught myself on the seat in front of me.

"Beth? What's going on?" I wriggled again trying to

move my hands. "Why the hell are my hands taped together?"

I finally got myself upright and realized both my hands and my feet were duct-taped together. My original panic multiplied by a hundred.

"So many questions. I think I liked it better when you were passed out."

"Why are you doing this? I didn't have anything to do with you getting fired. I promise."

"Fired. I don't give a fuck about that stupid job."

"Why would you do this?" I asked and tried to pry my hands apart, but the duct tape wouldn't budge.

Duct tape. I remembered the conversation I had with Nick about using tape to tie up Beth. The irony wasn't lost on me that I was the one taped by Beth. Nick. He'd know I was missing when he got home, and I wasn't there. Or would he? What if he thought I'd changed my mind about going to his place and went back to mine? Would he look for me?

"Remember when you woke up in the hospital and I came to visit you?" she asked.

I'd never forget the visit. I'd only just woken up from the attack when Beth had appeared at my bedside. At first, she acted like a concerned friend. Careful and cautious with me, then out of nowhere she'd turned into a cold-hearted bitch. That was the first time she'd commented on my face, and how sad it was that I was now ugly and no man would ever come near me again. Yeah, damn right I remembered.

"Yes," I answered.

"You know what's so funny? You have no idea how close you came to dying."

"I think I do."

"No. Not in the alley. In the hospital. I came in ready to finish what I'd started. I couldn't have you running to the police and blabbing. But when you woke up and cried your eyes out to me and hugged me, I realized you had no memory of what had happened, and it wasn't worth the risk of killing you with all the nurses in and out. Not to mention, scrubbing the hospital's server would be too difficult, there'd be footage of my visit. I let you live Meadow. And you know what I got in return?"

What the hell was she talking about? Let me live? No. No way. Beth was a crazy bitch, but there was no way... was there?

"I'm confused, Beth."

"I'll tell you what I got. You talking shit about me behind my back. Every fucking day, you talked shit about Queen Bitch, douchebaggette, twat-waffle, any of those ring a bell?" she yelled.

Shit goddammit. She had my phone and was

reading my messages to Veronica Venus. Fuck. She was right; there was about five years' worth of messages. Wait. If she had my phone, Nick would find me.

"Five goddamned years." She held a phone up shaking it, the shiny purple case reflecting the dim light in the car.

"That's not my phone," I lamely said.

"No shit. Do you think I'm dumb enough to bring your phone so your FBI boyfriend can track it? How stupid do you think I am? And the office security feeds have been erased for the last seven days. No one's going to find you Meadow."

Wait, then how was she reading my messages to Veronica Venus?

"Did you clone my phone?" I asked.

"Why the hell would I waste my time doing that? The only two people you talk to are your mother and me. You really should've been more careful about browsing the internet on company computers. Message boards, online shopping, plastic surgeons to try and fix your ugly-ass face. All on company time on the company computer."

Me?

What the fuck! I'd never spoken to Beth on my cell phone.

"You? What are you talking about?"

"Do you know how nauseating it is listening to you cry and whine every day about how bad your life is? How lonely you are? How your life was stolen from you? You cannot possibly know how many times I wanted to tell you to shut the fuck up. Flirty sluts like you who think they can bat their eyelashes and steal other people's husbands are the ones that ruin lives. No one ever thinks about the wife at home, trying to make her husband happy. Giving everything of themselves for nothing. Nothing. All it takes is some skank in a short skirt and you lose everything. Why wasn't I good enough?"

Holy shit, she'd lost her mind. The woman was batshit crazy, obviously, I mean I was duct-taped in the back of her car, but she was completely off her rocker. I had no idea what she was talking about, and I was afraid to ask.

"They deserved it. Every one of them. Fucking whores out trolling for men not caring if they're taken or not. You got lucky, I was sloppy the first time and impatient. I took you out back too soon, and you were still able to talk. Never made that mistake again."

The mother of all lightning bolts hit me. Jesus fuck. It was her!

"Why are you doing this to me?" I had to find a way out of this - she was going to kill me. I had no doubt I was about to be dragged out of the car and stabbed in the face until there was nothing left. I'd read the reports; I knew what she'd done.

Please, God, Nick! I didn't want him to see me dead in the alley with my face like that. He'd blame himself.

"Why not you?"

"You're right. Why not me? I'm begging you not to leave me here. Drive to another city and dump my body. Don't do it here. I won't scream this time, I promise. Just please, I'm begging you not here."

"You don't get a say. You're not in charge, I am. This is my way."

"Please Beth," I tried again.

"Now you want to be nice? Well, fuck you. We're done talking - it's time."

I tried to struggle and stop her from getting me out of the car. I screamed and yelled and tried to bite her. Nothing worked. I was out of the backseat and on the cold, dirty asphalt of the alley.

"Stay still," she told me as I thrashed around as much as I could with my limbs bound.

"Not here. Please, Beth!"

I kicked and knocked the knife out of her hand, but it wasn't hard enough because it was back in her hand

and headed straight for me. I twisted again, and the familiar burn of her blade sliced my leg.

"God damn, I fucking hate you. Always such a pain in the ass, stay fucking still."

Her knife caught me again, and I cried out. I was exhausted from the exertion. Not here, please God, don't let Nick find me. I didn't think I could keep this up much longer. Her arm went back, and I strained to move my head, but there was no way to get out of the way.

I'm so sorry Nick.

The low menacing growl pulled Beth's attention from me, and I rolled to my side in time to see Beth stick her knife in Sally as the dog jumped at Beth knocking her to the ground.

No! I tried to scream, but no words came out. Please don't let that be Sally. There had to be strays running the streets, right? Not Sally. Please, not her.

"Don't move," a man yelled as Beth struggled to her feet. "Beth Stevens, you're under arrest."

There was so much commotion I didn't know what to do. There was nothing I could do but lie there as men yelled at Beth to put her hands up and move away from me. I didn't know where her knife went. Would she still kill me in front of the police?

"Please Beth," I cried.

"Shut up. This is all your fault. All of it. If you would've kept your mouth shut, none of this would've happened."

"It's over, Beth," a woman's voice joined the male voices.

Beth didn't get the chance to answer. Out of nowhere, she was tackled from behind, her head hitting the ground with a sickening thud. At the same time, I was grabbed under my armpits and pulled away from a struggling Beth. She was screaming obscenities and threatening to kill me.

My body tensed, and fight or flight set in; I fought against the hold, trying to break free.

"It's me, Red. Relax baby; you're safe."

Nick.

"Where's Sally?" I asked.

"Let me worry about you right now."

"No! I'm fine. Please, Nick. Help her; she saved my life. Go to her."

"Joel's got her. Let me cut you free and check your leg."

"Please, Nick. She saved me."

He didn't answer. The tape binding my wrists and ankles were cut, and Nick rubbed my arms. He called for a medic, and soon a man and a woman joined us. Neither of us spoke, but he never took his eyes from mine. I heard the man tell Nick I needed to get to a hospital. Nick nodded and held my hand while I was loaded into the ambulance. I was surprised when he climbed in after me. I thought he'd need to stay behind with the police, but he never let go.

"I'm sorry I drank the coffee. I was so stupid. I'm so sorry I killed Sally."

Nick hung his head, and the thin leash that was holding me together snapped when the first tear fell from his eye.

It was all my fault.

25

Fly or drive?

THE HOSPITAL WAS SWARMING with police when the ambulance pulled into the ER bay. The back doors of the rig were pulled open, and Meadow's stretcher was flanked by police on both sides as we were escorted to a private room usually reserved for chemical contamination or communicable diseases. The threat of Beth Stevens was now contained; however, the media would be surrounding the hospital like flies on shit. I was grateful the local PD was doing what they could to keep them at bay.

The doctor came in, and the rapid-fire questions began. She was taking Meadow's vitals and inquiring about past medical history. Through it all I sat there stone-faced, unable to give Meadow the reassurance she wanted.

I'd failed her.

I was still failing her.

I couldn't stop the replay reel of Meadow thrashing around on the ground. One second later. That was all it would've taken. If Sally hadn't gotten loose and charged Beth, Meadow could've died. I could do nothing; there was no time for me to get to her.

Sally!

Jesus fuck, the dog saved my girl, not me. I didn't do a damn thing. And all Meadow was worried about was if Sally was okay. Then she apologized to me for taking coffee from Beth.

My phone vibrated, and I pulled it from my pocket.

Joel: Sally is at the emergency vet clinic on 12th. Updates to follow. How's Meadow?

Me: Thanks. With the doc now.

"You're a lucky lady, Meadow. Two lacerations. One I'm going to suture, the other I'll Dermabond. I want to get your thigh cared for before we clean your back. I can Steri-Strip a few of the deeper cuts. Your back is going to be sore. I'm more concerned with the abrasions becoming infected than I am about the clean incisions on your leg. Your back will need to be washed twice a day with anti-bacterial soap, you'll have a beta-dine ointment to use as well. I'm going to give you a round of IV antibiotics now and write you a ten-day script. Any questions?"

"No," Meadow answered.

"Yes," I countered. "She was drugged with ketamine. What are the side effects?"

"I was told. Ketamine is a dissociative anesthetic; it is short lasting, meaning the effect will wear off quickly. As the drug leaves the system, reactions vary from high blood pressure, muscle spasms, hallucinations, and extreme agitation. The flip side is low blood pressure and decreased breathing. Meadow isn't presenting any adverse side effects," the doctor informed me.

"What about a concussion? We don't know if she hit her head," I argued.

"I'm fine, Nick." Meadow grabbed my hand and I fought not to jerk it away.

"We don't know that," I said.

"Agent Clark. I understand your concern. I can assure you we will be observing Miss Holiday closely over the next few hours, but as of now, it's my belief she'll be home in her bed tonight with pain meds to manage any discomfort."

"Nick?"

Fuck. I couldn't take Meadow's tears; I needed a minute to regain my composure.

"I'll be right back. I need to check in with the guys," I lied, pulling my hand free.

I didn't miss the look of disappointment when I left the exam room. I also didn't miss the sound of Meadow's sobs.

I yanked my phone back out of my pocket and dialed the one person I knew could help. I didn't bother with the time, because they wouldn't care. Day or night didn't matter.

"Hello?"

"Sorry to bother you. You gotta minute?" I asked.

"Always. What's wrong?"

"I fucked up." I tried to hide the hitch in my voice, but nothing escaped my uncle's notice.

"We'll be there," he answered. No questions. No hesitation. I was a grown man, yet Nolan would rush to my side if needed.

"That's not necessary. I just need to talk," I told him.

"We'll talk. But first I need to know if it can wait the eight hours it will take me to drive or if I need a flight?"

Shit. I shouldn't have called.

"Really, you don't need to come."

"Bullshit. Fly or drive?"

"Drive," I told him.

"Great, I'll book a flight. Now, tell me what's wrong?"

Did he not hear me tell him to drive?

Instead of arguing, I broke down and told him about Meadow, and what I could about the investigation, and how tonight had played out. By the end, I thought I was going to throw up. I still couldn't wrap my head around how close Meadow came to dying.

"Fuck, Nicholas. That was a close call. Glad to hear Meadow's safe. You did good. Proud of you."

"Did you hear what I said? I fucked up. I missed the fucking big flashing sign over Beth's head. It's my fault."

"Yeah. I heard everything you said. I also know that you have your head up your ass. Nothing, I repeat nothing that bitch did, was your fault. Meadow is safe. End of story."

"My head's not..."

"Nick, you're gonna listen to me carefully. Go back to your woman. Grab her and hold tight."

"I can't even look at her; I fucked up so bad. I don't know how she doesn't hate me."

"Fuck," he cursed, and I heard the phone being

pulled away from his face before a muffled "Hey Lenox? Grab the guys, wheels up in twenty."

"Nolan, that's not necessary I don't need everyone coming up here. I'm fine."

"No, boy, you're not fine. You're getting ready to make the biggest mistake of your life. Listen. To. Me. Go to Meadow. Do not say anything to her until we get there. Hold her and give her whatever she needs. I need you to fight like hell not to run away. We'll be there as soon as we can."

"How'd you know I was gonna run?" I asked.

"Because I almost did when your Aunt Reagan lost her fucking kidney because I had my head up my ass, denying to myself and everyone else I was in love with her. Do you want to know about fucking up? Boy, you can't hold a candle to me. I'll be there. You hold tight." He disconnected before I could ask him what he meant.

I knew the story about my Aunt Reagan getting taken and being held on an abandoned oil rig that was being used as a black-market organ trafficking hospital, but I didn't know my uncle had felt responsible. Reagan and my uncle had just started dating when I moved in with them. When she'd moved to Florida to start a job it sucked, I missed her, and Nolan thought he hid it, but he was heartbroken.

What kind of pussy was I calling my uncle for help while I stood in the hallway of a hospital crying like a fucking baby?

I sent off a text to Joel asking about Sally. Still no updates, she was in surgery. Please, God, do not let Sally die!

When I walked back into the room, my betrayal smacked me dead center in my chest. Meadow was lying on a hospital bed clutching the sheet at her side while the doctor stitched her leg - alone. Not only was I weak, but I was a total douchebag leaving her the way I did. I broke my promise to her. I gave her my word she'd never be alone again. Yet there she was folded into herself without me by her side.

"Hey." I slid next to her and pried her fingers off the fabric and brought them up to my mouth, kissing each of them. "I'm sorry."

Meadow's red-rimmed eyes came to mine, and she tried to smile. God, she was killing me. She was the one that was attacked but she was reassuring me.

"I'm..."

"Shhh, Red. Just rest. We'll talk later," I told her.

The doctor finished with the gashes on the thigh and rolled her to the side to wash the abrasions on her back. I stayed where I was and lowered my face to hers, so we were inches apart.

"I'm so proud of you. You were so damn brave, baby," I told her as the doctor continued to tend to her road rash.

"How did you find me?" she asked.

"We tracked one of Beth's phones."

"One of them? What do you mean?"

"It's not important. We'll talk about it when we get you home."

I wasn't prepared to tell her that Beth was Veronica Venus; and I didn't think Meadow was emotionally ready for another blow. That type of betrayal was crushing. Meadow had poured her heart out to the woman who'd been behind all her pain. It made me sick thinking about it.

Four hours later the team, minus Joel who was still with Sally, had gathered outside Meadow's hospital room. I'd gotten a reprieve, and Kilby let me write my after-action report at the hospital. He also postponed my interview, so I didn't have to leave Meadow.

"Good work today," Kilby said as he prepared to leave. I gritted my teeth, stopping myself from telling him there was nothing good about Beth Stevens getting her filthy hands on Meadow.

Mandy's hand went to my shoulder and gave it a squeeze. "I agree. Strong work. Meadow is safe, and Beth is behind bars."

"You ready to take her home?" Detective Lance said when he approached.

"Yes. She's been released; we're waiting on your okay," I told him.

As predicted, the outside of the hospital was crawling with media. It was a madhouse outside, and we'd been planning our escape without being noticed.

"I've arranged for her to be taken by ambulance back to Firehouse 15. There is an unmarked car already there waiting to take you home. I'll follow the ambulance in my car to make sure the rig isn't being followed," he explained.

"Thank you, much appreciated."

"It's the least I can do for being such an asshole. I was wrong and doubted you and damn if your profile wasn't spot on. I won't be making that mistake again." Detective Lance offered his hand to Kilby, who graciously took his hand in a brief shake and nod.

"You'll have our reports in the next day or two," Kilby told him, then turned to us. "Any word on Sally? Christ Almighty when that dog jumped over the seat and darted out of the car I didn't know what to expect. Her jumping into Beth Stevens was not what I expected. Though she *is* yours; I should've known she'd go off reservation."

The team chuckled, and I did my best to smile though I knew it had to look more like a grimace.

"Joel said she made it through surgery, but the vet said it didn't look good. I'd appreciate no one saying anything to Meadow. She's torn up about what happened, and I'm afraid what the news will do to her."

The team gave their agreement, and Lance escorted us back through the ER to an awaiting ambulance. Meadow's gurney was quickly loaded, and the rig took off.

26

The uncles

"HOW COULD I not have known you were so infuriating? And possibly the most stubborn man alive?" I whined.

"Me? Stubborn? You do remember you were in the hospital a few hours ago, right? And... don't roll your eyes at me Meadow."

"Nick. I can walk to the bathroom. You don't need to carry me every time I have to pee."

"The doctor said not to put pressure on your leg," he reminded me for the tenth time. The fluids I'd received at the ER were running through me, and I had to pee every five minutes, which meant Nick was carrying me back and forth to the bathroom every five minutes.

"She said *much* pressure. I can limp to use the bathroom."

This time Nick rolled his eyes at me and ignored my protest when he sat me on the couch. When we got home, he'd put me to bed, and I dozed, but a horrible nightmare had woken me up. Nick held me until I stopped crying and now I didn't want to go back to sleep. The painkillers were making it hard to keep my eyes open, but fear of reliving my attack was a great motivator. So was the grief I saw on Nick's face when he rocked me, apologizing over and over that he allowed Beth to get to me.

It didn't matter how many times I told him it wasn't his fault; he kept saying it was. I'd do anything to keep the guilt and sadness from his eyes. He'd saved me, and I couldn't understand why he couldn't see that. Him and Sally. I knew he was keeping secrets from me. For one he told me Sally was out of surgery, but instead of relief, there was trepidation. When I questioned him, he brushed it off. He said he didn't blame me for Sally getting hurt, but I didn't believe him. It was my fault. Beth had stabbed her because she was trying to save me. Sally took the blow that was meant for me. How could Nick not hate me? Then there was the issue of Beth's second phone, and why he was being so secretive about it. I couldn't figure out what the big deal was. I mean, sure it was weird she had two phones, but it's not unheard of. Something wasn't right. I started to tell him that Beth must've hacked into my phone or computer because she'd read the messages I'd sent to Veronica Venus. Then there were her weird ramblings about listening to me bitch and complain. That conversation was shut down too, but not before he stumbled on his words and turned very uncomfortable. I didn't understand why, and I didn't like it.

"Would you like something to drink?" he asked, ignoring my reminder.

"No, thank you. I'm not drinking anything else that will make me need to pee more until you let me use the bathroom on my own."

His lips twitched, and his right eyebrow pulled up. "Is that so?"

The first sign of a ghost of a smile since he'd found me.

"Yes, it is." I smiled at him. "I wish you'd talk to me."

"We are talking."

"Don't be daft. You know what I'm saying."

"Daft?" Nick chuckled. "I've been called many things, daft isn't one of them."

"Stop changing the subject," I groaned.

Nick sighed and brushed my hair over my shoulder, exposing my scar and gently trailing his finger over it. "The details aren't important. What is important is, you're here safe and Beth is locked in a cage where she belongs."

"They're important to me."

The knock on the door interrupted his response, and he was all too happy to excuse himself to see who was there. It was strange not having Sally here; her crate and dog bed sat empty in the corner. If Nick refused to give me answers, I'd find them myself. He'd mentioned the name of the clinic she was being treated at; I didn't know if privacy laws pertained to vets like they did doctors, but I was going to find out. One way or another I would get the truth and not only about Sally. It was frustrating, I had all the information, but I couldn't put it together.

Nick walked back into the living room, followed by four men, all with matching scowls. I tried to scoot back into the couch and make myself as small as possible. The man that had walked in behind Nick quickly masked his frown and his face went blank.

"Meadow. These are my uncles: Nolan, Lenox, Levi, and Jasper."

Well, that explained it, Nick Clark came from good stock. The grey and fine wrinkles only added to their appeal.

Can you say – silver fox?

Sweet Jesus. Of all times for me to meet his uncles, I was a mess. I tried to shuffle to stand, and all five men lunged at me.

"Red," Nick warned.

The other four all made similar warning sounds. Sheesh, now I understood where Nick got that too.

The glare I leveled at Nick did not deter. "Don't cut your eyes at me. You're not supposed to put pressure on your leg."

"*Much.* Much pressure. I think I can manage to stand for two seconds to meet your family. Either you can help me stand, or I'll do it myself, and if I bust a stitch and you tell me I told you so, I swear to all things holy I will... scream." I finished lamely.

"Christ," one of the men said.

"It is like deja vu," another added.

"Apple didn't roll far from the tree."

"'Bout damn time he found her."

Nick's eyes narrowed on the men. "You're not

helping. None of you. She needs to stay off that goddamn leg."

What was going on? Why was he so upset?

"Nick?" He looked from his uncles to me. "I'll stay seated. But I want it on record; I'm doing so not because I don't think I should walk, I'm doing it because it seems to matter to you. I promise you I'm fine. And don't think because I'm giving in now, means you're gonna carry me to the bathroom again."

"Thank you."

At least he had the decency to look embarrassed about being an overbearing jerk.

"It's nice to meet you all," I told the men.

They all returned my greeting, introducing themselves again. Nolan and Nick looked almost identical, and when Nick explained that Clark, as he's called by the others, was his blood and the rest all served in the Army with him and were honorary uncles, it made sense.

Clark made himself at home, getting everyone drinks. When he handed me a bottle of water, Nick stopped him.

"She's on strike, refusing to drink until I allow her to walk."

I got a round of *good for you*. Clark slapped Nick

on the back and muttered something about me fitting right in with his aunts.

I didn't want to think about what that meant. If more people were on their way over, I was getting up and getting dressed. Nick could throw a temper tantum all he wanted; I was not meeting the women in his family looking like this.

27

Alive and breathing

"YOU'RE gonna give yourself a stroke if you don't calm down," my uncle told me.

I loved my uncles, but I was happy Lenox, Jasper, and Levi were all getting ready to leave to have dinner with the director to discuss some upcoming training contracts. Now that they'd retired from the Army, they owned a huge facility where they offered comprehensive firearms instruction and scenario-based training to a variety of government agencies. They'd never been short on contracts since they'd opened their doors; men with their specialized skillset were in high demand.

I didn't need them all ganging up on me again, telling me Meadow looked like she was getting ready to stab me and they'd hold me down, so she had a clear target.

"You don't understand." I gritted my teeth, trying not to lose patience with the men who had raised me.

"I don't?" Nolan's face turned to stone, his stance widened, and his arms crossed over his wide chest, a pose that used to scare the shit out of me when I was a teenager.

"How could you? I fucked up. I was so caught up in her that I didn't see what was right in front of my face. She almost died. One more minute and she wouldn't be here. Do you know what that feels like?"

"I do. When I found your aunt on that oil rig, she'd already lost a fucking kidney and half her liver. The motherfucker had opened her up and taken an organ, Nicholas. Do you want to know what he was selling next? Her goddamn eyes. She was prepped and ready to be butchered again when we got there. So, yes, son, I think I understand exactly what you're feeling. You were there, you knew how I felt about Reagan, but I was trying to play it cool, and let her go. You wanna know why I didn't stop her from leaving and moving to Florida? Pride. I was too afraid she'd turn me down and move after I told her how I felt. And my poor man-ego was afraid of rejection. I let her go. I wasn't there to protect her. *She* almost died. They both almost died.

But neither of them did. Meadow is alive and breathing."

Shit. I felt like a complete asshole. I was only eleven when Reagan was taken. My uncle was scared to death even though he tried his best to hide it from me. Everyone was. When she came home, no one talked to me about the specifics. I was a kid, and my uncles did their best to shield me from anything that would upset me.

"The only thing that mattered to me was that she was breathing when I found her. I must've repeated it a thousand times in my head – *as long as you're breathing I can love you through anything.* The whole time she was in the hospital, all I needed was for her to keep breathing. The rest? The scars, both physical and emotional – we'd love her through them. Her night-mares – I'd hold her. It didn't matter. None of it did."

"She wants to know the details," I told him.

"So tell her," Jasper spoke for the first time.

"What? Why? She doesn't need to know," I countered.

"You're wrong. She does. Your aunt blackmailed me into telling her what happened when I found her. She refused to move in with us until I told her what happened on the oil platform. I dodged every time she asked me, until one night in bed she held my ass to the fire and demanded I tell her everything," Nolan explained.

"She's not ready. I'm doing the right thing," I argued.

"No." Lenox started. "You're not ready. And that I know something about. I spent twelve years thinking I was doing the right thing, and another nine months after that fighting a losing battle. It almost lost me Lily and Carter."

Levi had been the only one not to speak up, but by the look of condemnation on his face, I knew I was about to get a dressing down.

"You're wasting time, and all of us standing here can tell you, time is not your friend. Man up, and tell her what she wants to know. When she breaks under the weight, hold her up. The woman in there loves you, don't waste it because of some misplaced guilt. There was nothing you could've done differently that would've prevented Beth from hurting Meadow. If you keep holding on to that notion, there will be no room left for Meadow."

"What's going on?" Meadow asked as she limped into the living room.

Levi's hand on my shoulder halted my reprimand. "You're gonna have to learn to pick your battles. She's stronger than you think. And you handling her with kid gloves is not helping. You can only push her so far before you're on the begging end of this relationship. Trust me, it sucks."

"Nothing, sweetheart. Come and sit down. We were just getting ready to leave for dinner," Nolan answered.

"You're going too?" I asked.

"Yeah. Meadow, Nick has some stuff he needs to tell you; we'll give you privacy."

My own fucking uncle threw me under the bus.

Goddammit to hell.

28

Veronica Venus

"WHY DO YOU KEEP APOLOGIZING? It's not your fault."

I was trying to be patient, but now I was getting annoyed. Nick had apologized no less than five times in the last thirty minutes since his uncles left.

"I should've gotten to you sooner."

"Really? How? With your psychic abilities? You guys found me; that's all that matters."

Sheesh. Enough with the guilt already!

"She drugged you, and…"

"Stop. Enough. I know what she did Nick. I was there. I drank the coffee. I am the one who should've known better than to drink anything she gave me. She probably spit in it too. She hated me and didn't hide it. Why I thought it was a good idea to take anything from her is *my* mistake. Now, please just tell me what her second phone had to do with how you found me, and why it's a big deal?"

"Fuck, Red. You remember how she told you she had listened to you whine about your life for the past five years, and she knew everything you told Veronica Venus?"

"Yeah. She had to have hacked my phone or something."

"No, baby, Beth is Veronica Venus."

"What?"

How was that possible? Veronica Venus lived in South Dakota. I met her after my attack on a message board. That didn't make any sense.

"Beth was pretending to be a survivor so she could get close to you and keep tabs in case you remembered anything. We were also able to isolate messages from Veronica Venus and pings on her cellphone that she had been following you a long time."

"That's not possible. How would she know what message board I belonged to, or my handle?"

"When did you start messaging with Veronica Venus?" he asked.

"I don't know; after my attack, I joined the message board."

"Right, but when did VV21 pop up on the message board? Had you gone back to work?"

Holy shit.

"She said I should've been more careful using company computers. When I went back to work sometimes on my lunch break, I would sit at my desk and log in to the message board."

"Why would she do that?" I cried. "Oh God, Nick, I told her everything."

I didn't care that Beth knew I'd called her names behind her back. If I'd been strong enough at the time, I would've said them to her face. It was all the other stuff I told her. I'd spilled my guts to the woman who hurt me, all of my thoughts and feelings about never having children, not feeling worthy of love or a man, and how I felt less of a woman. Oh, my God. I poured my heart out thinking she was my best friend; she knew everything about me. Everything.

"I'm sorry, Red, come here." Nick tried to pull me closer to him, but I recoiled. I didn't want him touching me, or feeling sorry for me - poor stupid Meadow.

"Don't. Please just leave me alone."

"No, Red..."

"Leave Nick. I don't need your fucking pity."

"I don't pity you." Then he sighed. "This is why I didn't want to tell you yet. You needed more time."

"More time for what? More time for you to laugh at me about what an idiot I am?"

"Enough. You're not an idiot and I would never fucking laugh at you." Nick's face had turned to stone, and his voice was rough with anger.

"Great. Just great. Did everyone on your team read the messages?"

"Meadow, listen to me, it wasn't like that. No one was reading the messages to invade your privacy. We were simply trying to find clues as to where she would've taken you. Then she powered on the phone and Kristy was able to ping your location."

"So, everyone knows how weak and pathetic I am. Whining and crying to my imaginary online friend about how lonely I was, how I'd never have a husband or baby, how I was falling in love with you. Oh, my God, they saw what I told Veronica Venus, ugh, Beth, about our first date."

"No one sees you that way, and no one cares what you told that bitch. I promise you they were not reading the messages to gossip. All we wanted to do was find you."

"Please just leave. I need some time to myself," I begged.

"No way, Red. I'm not letting you sit in here by yourself."

I needed him to go. I was embarrassed and ashamed. I couldn't bear to look at him. How could I have been so stupid to tell my most inner thoughts to a stranger? So, I did the cruelest thing I could think of – the unimaginable.

"I don't want you here. This is all your fault. Now leave me alone."

I regretted the words immediately. Nick recoiled and hung his head before he looked back at me with more pain and shame than I'd ever seen in a person's eyes. I did that, and to further twist the knife in my heart, I did it on purpose, so he would leave me to wallow alone in my self-hatred. I lashed out trying to make him hate me so I could in turn hate myself more. I didn't deserve Nick. I was broken and weak. He needed a woman who was his equal, not someone who had nothing to offer.

I was destined to be alone the rest of my life.

29

Ugly regret

"HOW LONG HAVE you been sitting there?" Nolan asked.

"Long enough for her to cry herself to sleep and my ass to go numb," I told him.

"Come on, let's take a walk."

"I can't leave. If she has a nightmare, I need to be here."

"Levi will stand guard. You need a break."

I relented only because I knew my uncle and he wouldn't stop pestering me until I did as he asked. We walked out to the living room, and Levi went down the hall, taking my place standing guard outside the door. I'd helplessly listened as Meadow sobbed until she'd finally fallen asleep. I was completely lost and didn't know what I was supposed to do next. She blamed me, too. Was I supposed to drive her home when she woke up and let her recuperate on her own? Make her stay and suffer having to look at the man who almost got her killed?

"What happened?" Jasper asked.

I told Nolan, Jasper, and Lenox about the conversation I had with Meadow and how she'd finally admitted that she blamed me.

"You know she didn't mean what she said, she was trying to protect herself and push you away," Lenox said.

"I don't know why you think that, but you're wrong. You didn't see the hate in her eyes. She meant every word."

"I know I'm right because I did the same thing to Lily when she first came back into my life. We'd spent about two weeks together. They were perfect; she was perfect. Then fear and self-doubt crept in, and I didn't believe I deserved her. The team got a call-out, and I used it as an excuse to break Lily's heart. I needed her to hate me, so I could walk away. I lied right to her face and told her I didn't love her. When she called me out, I told her all she was to me was a good fuck. You cannot imagine the disgust I felt saying those words to the woman I adored. I understand why Meadow pushed you away. She doesn't think she deserves love."

I believed that Lenox thought he was right. And once again, more information about my uncle's past was coming to light. I had no idea he and Aunt Lily had a rocky start. However, he was wrong about my situation with Meadow.

"I don't know what to do now," I admitted. "She blames me; I blame myself. What the hell do I do."

"You wanna cut her loose?" Jasper asked.

"Fuck no. But I don't think I have another option."

"You always have another option. Pull your head out of your ass and fight for her. Both of you are hurting. Love is not earned, it is given. You need to remind her your love is unconditional and without exception. Do not let her dwell on the past. It will eat her up until there is nothing left but ugly regret."

I was stunned into silence. I couldn't believe that my big badass uncles were standing in my living room talking about love and giving me advice about my woman.

"That sounds all too familiar," Nolan chuckled.

"What does?" I asked.

"You think you're the first man to have woman trouble? This is not our first rodeo, son. We all struggled, we all fucked up, we all needed the help of our brothers to help us see the beauty standing in front of us. We know we're right because we've lived this. All four of us have needed the help of the others to get our shit straight. So, for fuck sake, you've given your woman enough time to lick her wounds. Now you need to go back in there, wrap her up and no matter what she throws at you, remember – you love her without exception. And I promise you what is on the other side of this is a beauty you cannot fully comprehend. Ride the storm, Nick. You've got this – we've got this."

Nolan patted my shoulder, giving me a renewed strength. I didn't realize how desperately I had needed my uncles, my family, until that moment. Damn, I missed them. Without needing any further encouragement, I walked down the hall, thanked Levi, and opened my bedroom door. Meadow was lying on her side, eyes open, staring at the wall. When the hinge creaked, her eyes came to mine, but she quickly averted them. She looked so fucking small curled up into a ball; I'd screwed up - again. I never should've left her alone in her misery. It shouldn't have mattered what she said to me; I should've stayed and held her.

That was a mistake I'd never make again.

I crawled into bed behind her and pulled her back to my front and wrapped my arms around her.

A long while later she broke the silence. "I shouldn't have said it was your fault. I didn't mean it. It was rotten and mean and... horrible. I was just so embarrassed; I didn't want you to see me like that. It was wrong, and it will never happen again."

I kissed the back of her head and remained quiet. I'd let her talk if she needed but I only wanted to hold her, let her know that I was strong enough to shoulder the burden.

"Do you want kids?" she whispered.

"Yes." Then I quickly reminded her. "We'll adopt. There's a child out there that needs us. You will be a mom."

"It wasn't your fault. I know you did everything you could to find me and I can't tell you how grateful I am that you came when you did."

"I was so scared," I admitted. "The whole time she had you I was going out of my mind. The entire day, actually. Something didn't feel right. Sally knew; she was pacing and on alert. When we pulled up to the alley and heard you screaming, she jumped over the center console, out the open driver's side door and took off to protect you. I owe a dog a debt of gratitude I can never repay. She saved your life."

"Do we get to keep her?"

"Bet your ass. She isn't going anywhere."

30

A thousand deaths

"ARE YOU READY?" I asked for the twentieth time.

"Hold your horses," Nick yelled back from the kitchen.

It had been four days, and Sally was ready to come home. Nick's uncles left yesterday. I was sad to see them go. After some of the shock wore off from Beth's attempt to kill me, it was nice to get to know them. They were every bit as protective as Nick was. It was easy to see the four men had raised Nick to be the man he was; caring, brave, and considerate. I didn't know if you could teach someone to be good-looking, but if you could, they did that, too. Holy smokes Nick's uncles were gorgeous. It was no wonder Nick had a baseball team full of cousins. We'd made plans to go to Georgia when I was fully recovered so I could meet the rest of the tribe, as Nick called them. I couldn't wait.

Nick and I had spent a lot of time together over the last few days lying in bed talking, telling each other about our childhoods. He'd mentioned his mom, Stephanie, a few times but never elaborated much. I was shocked when he told me that Stephanie was married to his uncle Nolan and had an affair with Nolan's brother, Nicholas, while Nolan was on deployment. Nicholas was also in the Army and had deployed soon after the affair was discovered. Sadly, he died when his helicopter was hit by a RPG two months later. Nick had never seen a picture of his dad until he moved in with Nolan when his mom was arrested on vehicular manslaughter charges. She was sentenced to two life sentences and died in prison of liver failure. Nolan and Reagan adopted Nick when he was twelve. He said he could barely remember a time when he didn't have them.

"Okay, ready." Nick walked into the living room and my mouth watered. Damn, he was sexy. It didn't matter what he was wearing – a suit for work, athletic gear to go to the gym, or jeans and a tee like he was wearing now; he looked mighty fine.

"I forgot to ask, how did your conversation with Alexandra go?"

"Good. She completely agreed that Sally shouldn't be separated from you. She's going to pair Gabe with a new dog."

I felt horrible that Gabe was going to have to wait to be paired with a new dog, but I couldn't imagine Sally not being with us.

"But he'll still get one, right?"

"Yes. Alexandra said she already has the perfect dog in mind. A retired Belgian Malinois named Dottie. Her handler's wife is having twins, and there are complications. He'll only let Dottie go if Alex can pair her with one of her vets. So, it's perfect. Malinois require a lot of attention, especially one that is a retired working dog. Dottie will keep Gabe active, and that is one of Alex's goals."

"Knowing that makes me feel better. I hate thinking that Gabe would be without a companion."

———

"OH MY GOD. NICK!"

Sally looked bad. She had something the vet called flail chest. Part of Sally's broken ribs had been detached and had caused pressure on her lungs. The bruising on her lungs made it difficult to breathe and almost killed her; that and Beth's stab had ruptured her spleen. All the beautiful fur down her belly had been shaved, and there was an angry red incision held together by staples. I hobbled over to the dog bed the vet had laid out for Sally.

"We didn't kennel her," Dr. Steel explained. "I didn't want her anymore agitated than she already was without you." I tuned out the rest of what the doctor was saying and only heard Nick's half-growl half-grunt when I knelt in front of Sally to cuddle her, but he didn't dare stop me.

"Aren't we a pair. Now we'll match." Sally licked my face when I rubbed my cheek to her snoot. "You're such a good girl."

Her tail swooshed on the floor, and she tried to scoot toward me.

"Don't move baby girl." Uncaring how dirty the floor was in the Vet clinic, or my leg screaming in protest, I laid on my side next to Sally, carefully wrapped my arms around her and cried into her soft fur. "You saved me." Sally burrowed in and shoved her face into the crook of my neck. I was so thankful Sally was alive I couldn't stop crying.

"Are you girls ready to go home now?"

Nick had given me time with Sally while he spoke with the vet, making sure he understood how to care for her wounds. I grabbed the paperwork, and a bag of wound care supplies, while Nick carried Sally to his car and placed her in the backseat. I slid in next to her, not wanting to leave her side even for a minute.

It was the same when we pulled in front of Nick's. He carried her inside and laid her on the bed.

"Don't get used to this," Nick warned. "In a few days, she'll be back on her bed."

Sure, she would.

Nick was a big ol' softy, and he was just as grateful to Sally as I was. I didn't believe he wanted her more than an arm's length away either.

My leg was throbbing, and the scabs on my back itched like crazy. When I got into bed next to Sally, I tried to rub my back on the sheets to quell some of the discomfort.

"Lie on your side, I'll rub your back with some arnica gel," Nick offered.

I should've known he wouldn't miss my scratching.

"You're too good to me. That would be wonderful. It itches so bad now."

"You know, it's only going to get worse. The more the scrapes heal, the itchier they'll be."

"Thanks for reminding me. I'll have to use a door jamb or a brush to itch."

"Or, you could move in here, and I can scratch them for you."

"Move in?"

My insides fluttered, and my heartrate picked up. Move in? Holy shit. Were we ready to live together? Maybe he meant while I was healing.

"Yeah, you know, pack up your apartment and drive it over here," he laughed.

I elbowed him in the ribs, and his laughter died on a grunt.

"Is it too soon?" I asked.

"Hell no. Do you love me?" his voice was unsure as he asked.

"Of course, I do."

"Then why wait?"

"Well..." I tried to think of a good reason, but I couldn't. Living here with Nick and Sally was a dream come true, something I never thought I'd have. Somehow this wonderful man had looked past my scars and loved me. What more could I ask for?

"I died a thousand deaths the day Beth had you. My heart felt like it was being ripped from my chest. Meadow, I know you're the one. I don't want to waste a day. I want my girls here, under my roof, where I can come home every day and love them. I want your clothes next to mine, us making coffee together in the morning, but most of all, I want to fall into bed every night with you where you're supposed to be – by my side. I love you, Red, and if you'll have me, one day soon I want to make you my wife and adopt all those kids I know you want. We'll fill our home full of love. You and me? There's nothing we can't do together."

I was speechless. I don't know what I'd done to deserve Nick and his unwavering love and support, but I wasn't going to squander it. If he was giving it, I was taking it, holding on to it, and protecting it. We had the foundation, the roots had taken hold, and I was basking in the glow. I would do everything in my power to make sure I nurtured and cherished our budding relationship until it grew so towering and unbreakable he'd never be sorry he chose me.

He pulled my shirt up and was spreading the cooling gel onto my back. I took a moment to enjoy his strong hands against my skin. When I looked at Sally, her sweet face resting on a pillow next to me, I knew I was home.

"I love you, Nicholas Clark."

"Does that mean you'll stay?"

"There is no place in the world I'd rather be."

The three of us laid in silence; there was no need to fill the moment with words. Peace had settled over the room, its weight heavy and comfortable—a promise for the future.

Home.

Becoming a man

FOUR YEARS LATER.

Nick's transfer had gone through, and he'd taken his wife home to Georgia.

Meadow had spent the last few months going back and forth between Virginia and Georgia to go house hunting with his aunts, who were all more than happy to help. They'd started dropping hints two years ago after he and Meadow had married that it was time to move home. The cousins missed him, and his uncles could use his help at their training facility. He wasn't ready to leave the FBI yet, but did agree it was time to go to Georgia and start a family of his own with Meadow.

After what seemed to be a hundred houses later, Meadow declared she'd found the perfect one, a four-bedroom with a huge yard for Sally and room for a swing set. What had Meadow so excited was it was in the same neighborhood as Nolan and Reagan's house. Nick liked that. He'd missed his family the last nine years he'd been away. Not that his family hadn't always been close by, his uncles were always at the ready to help when he needed. Thankfully, he'd only had to call on them once, when the weight of Meadow's near-death attack had left him close to breaking. He'd never be more grateful to the men for stopping him from what would've been his biggest regret. Luckily for Meadow and Nick, they knew no such regrets.

Nick watched from inside the house, through the wall of windows that gave a perfect unobstructed view of the backyard as Meadow threw Sally a ball. They were inseparable, Sally and Meadow, his girls. He couldn't wait to start welcoming children into their new home. They had an appointment with an adoption agency in a week. Nick was trying his hardest not to get his hopes up; it could take a long time for them to be accepted and then find a child to love. But he was more than ready.

There was a knock on the door, and Nick called out the back door to Meadow. "You ready?"

Before she could answer, voices filled the entryway and people started filing in.

"Yo! Now that you're home, you better get used to Jasper just walking in. After all these years, no one has been able to train him to wait for the door to be answered," Lenox said.

"Even after he's walked in on things he shouldn't see," Levi grouched.

"Gross," Adalyn Walker, Jasper and Emily's youngest daughter, said.

"Dad, why don't you just wait? It's totally rude," Delaney Walker, their eldest daughter, asked.

"Because he thinks it's funny to annoy people. Uncle Lenox said if he did it again he was going to put his foot in his ass. So, dad just does it more." Hadley Walker, Adalyn's twin, added.

"Hadley!" Emily Walker scolded her daughter.

"What? It's true. He said a bunch of other bad words I'm not saying. And Aunt Lily said she'd wash his mouth out with soap if he used the frick word in front of us again. Dad says it, like, all the time. You should wash his mouth out."

Jasper roared with laughter and patted his daughter on the head as he walked by her adding, "Sweetheart, if your mother tried to wash my mouth out with soap I'd bend her over my knee and spank her."

"Jasper!" Emily now chastised her husband, who was unfazed and winked at her.

"That is so gross. I know what that means!" Delaney whined. "Why can't I have normal parents? This is why I can't bring a boyfriend to the house."

Nick watched as two very interesting things happened. Carter Lenox, Lily and Lenox's eldest son, cut his eyes at Delaney, the possessive sound Carter made wouldn't have been missed if anyone had been paying attention. The other was Jasper stopped dead in his tracks, turned toward his very beautiful fifteen-year-old daughter, and he too made a sound that was of a possessive father. "You do not bring boyfriends to the house, because I will shoot them. And you can thank your mother for passing down her black hair, blue eyes, and sense of humor, three things that make teenage boys lose their minds. The first boy that knocks on my door will walk away with a limp."

"You are impossible," Delaney told Jasper.

Jasper was not wrong. His fifteen-year-old looked more like a twenty-year-old version of her very stunning mother. Jasper had three more after Delaney to worry about – all equally pretty.

Lily Lenox walked in with her son, Ethan,

following behind her; she had a tray of veggies, and Ethan was carrying a case of beer though he was nowhere near old enough to drink it.

Nick's younger brother, Jackson, and Quinn Walker came in holding a video game console, controllers, and cables. The two of them had been best friends since before they could walk. Then when they could, everyone wished they could lock them in a padded room together to contain the tornado they caused wherever they went. The two of them were trouble, and always up to something. Nick was afraid his brother was going to be in a world of hurt when Quinn grew up a little more, and other boys started to notice how beautiful she was. There would come a time when Quinn didn't want to build things with Jack anymore, and she'd notice the attention the boys were sure to give her.

"Where's your mom and dad?" Blake McCoy asked as she looked around the room for Reagan and Clark. Her husband Levi and their daughter Moira had already made their way to the kitchen to unload all the food they'd brought.

"I don't know, they told me to walk down here and they'd be up in a minute," Jack answered, helping himself to Nick's TV.

Nick and Meadow stood off to the side and smiled.

Controlled chaos, that was what Reagan had called it when the large group got together. It was perfect. Nick wouldn't want it any other way. This was how Nick had grown up – surrounded with love and laughter.

"Where's Jason and Kayla?" Meadow asked Emily about Nick's cousin and his fiancée.

"They'll be here soon. Jason forgot something at his house; they went to get it," Emily explained.

It took a while, but Nick had ushered everyone into the backyard where he and Meadow had set up tables for the food and coolers for the drinks. It was a beautiful day; the sun was shining, Sally was in dog heaven having six kids under the age of fifteen to chase around.

Meadow looked around the backyard and smiled. Perfect.

She loved their family. They were loud, they were hilarious, and they loved unconditionally. Nolan and Reagan tried to slip in unnoticed and sat at a table off to the side as if they weren't thirty minutes late.

Nick, Lenox, Jasper, and Levi glanced over at the couple and busted out laughing. Meadow wasn't sure what was so funny until she looked at Reagan. There was no doubt what the two of them had been doing with their time alone in their house.

Reagan's flushed cheeks turned a deep shade of

pink, and she smiled wide. "What? Can you blame me?"

Meadow couldn't stop herself; she too joined the men laughing. "Not one damn bit."

Nick tagged her around the waist and pulled her closer to him. "Really, Red?"

"What? There's something about the Clark men that inspires..."

"Don't finish that sentence." Nick laughed, and Meadow winked at Reagan.

"Damn, I knew she'd fit right in." Lenox smiled.

Meadow *had* fit right in. The moment they'd met her, she was accepted into the tribe and made one of them. She felt it four years ago, and she felt it now – there was no other place she'd rather be.

ETHAN LENOX NEEDED to talk to his parents. He'd been putting it off for the last week, and now the rock that had started in his stomach had turned into a boulder. He knew his parents loved him, but they were going to be so disappointed in him.

He'd fucked up, and he knew it.

He was sixteen-years-old, too young.

But he'd made up his mind.

"Mom. Dad. Can I talk to you a minute?"

Now was as good a time as any Ethan thought; better to just rip the scab off and bleed.

"What's wrong?" his mother asked.

"Fuck," his father muttered. Ethan was unable to hide his discomfort from his father. It wasn't often Ethan screwed up. He was a straight-A student and excelled at sports. His parents had instilled great respect in him; his coaches and teachers loved him. So did the cheerleaders, and that was where his current problem started. "As long as no one's knocked up, we can fix anything."

"Lenox." His mother slapped his father's shoulder.

Ethan tried to keep his face blank and stop his flinch, but it was too late. His father saw it.

"Shit," Lenox muttered.

The time had come for Ethan Lenox to become a man, years before he should've.

Ethan is up next in Chasing Honor

Protecting Olivia

Redeeming Violet

Recovering Ivy

Rescuing Erin

The Gold Team - Susan Stoker Universe

Brooks

Thaddeus

Kyle

Maximus

Declan

Blue Team - Susan Stoker Universe

Owen

Gabe

Myles

Kevin

Cooper

Garrett

The 707 Freedom Series

Free

Freeing Jasper

Finally Free

Freedom

The Next Generation (707 spinoff)

Saving Meadow

Chasing Honor

Finding Mercy

Claiming Tuesday

Adoring Delaney

Keeping Quinn

Taking Liberty

Triple Canopy

Damaged

Flawed

Imperfect

Tarnished

Tainted

Conquered

Shattered

Fractured

The Collective

Unbroken

Trust

AUDIO

Are you an Audio Fan?

Check out Riley's titles in Audio on Audible and iTunes

Gemini Group

Narrated by: Joe Arden and Erin Mallon

Red Team

Narrated by: Jason Clarke and Carly Robins

Gold Team

Narrated by: Lee Samuels and Maxine Mitchell

The 707 Series

Narrated by: Troy Duran and C. J. Bloom

More audio coming soon!

BE A REBEL

Riley Edwards is a USA Today and WSJ bestselling author, wife, and military mom. Riley was born and raised in Los Angeles but now resides on the east coast with her fantastic husband and children.

Riley writes heart-stopping romance with sexy alpha heroes and even stronger heroines. Riley's favorite genres to write are romantic suspense and military romance.

Don't forget to sign up for Riley's newsletter and never miss another release, sale, or exclusive bonus material.

Rebels Newsletter

Facebook Fan Group

www.rileyedwardsromance.com

facebook.com/Novelist.Riley.Edwards

instagram.com/rileyedwardsromance

bookbub.com/authors/riley-edwards

amazon.com/author/rileyedwards

www.ingramcontent.com/pod-product-compliance
Lightning Source LLC
Chambersburg PA
CBHW072027220726

48293CB00016B/472